Reading in the Bath

Reading in the Bath

Astrid Klemz

Bolero

First Published by Bolero Books 2002

Copyright © Astrid Klemz 2002

The moral right of the author has been asserted.

ISBN: 0-9538452-2-2

Reading In The Bath is a work of fiction. Names, characters and incidents are either the product of the author's imagination or are used entirely fictitiously.

A catalogue record for this book is available from the British Library.

Bolero Books is an imprint of Plum Tree Publishing Limited, Worcester, England, WR7 4NX

Printed and bound by
Creative Print & Design Wales (Ebbw Vale)

To Vincent

Contents

No Room in the Bedsit

I was heartily sick of Mr Chelsea. All he ever did was sit there looking miserable and he was sitting in my chair! I suppose I could just have sat down on top of him and ignored him, but whenever I did that, he disappeared and then he'd be back looking more miserable than ever, the minute I got up again.

I admit that as far as ghosts go he wasn't much bother. He didn't howl, or groan or take his head off in front of people. In fact he didn't do anything at all. He just sat in my chair.

It was a lovely chair, brown leather with buttons and in remarkably good condition for its age. I wanted to sit in it myself. It was the only real chair I had. I'd had to sit on the kitchen stool or the floor for weeks until the auction room came up with an armchair I could afford. I suppose I should have smelt a rat when it came up for sale for the third time and went for a price I could pay; but I didn't. I was just too glad to have a

1

comfortable armchair of my own to sit on at last.

But as soon as I got it home I found Mr Chelsea sitting in it. I knew his name was Mr Chelsea because he told me when I asked him and I knew he was a ghost because I could see right through him; right through his prissy little grey suit and his prim and proper old collar and tie.

When I asked him what he thought he was doing in my chair he replied, in that nitty-pritty voice of his, that it was his chair, and had been his chair since he set up home with Mabel in 1938. And as to what he was doing in it, why the answer was simplicity itself; he had been condemned to sit in it for so many thousands of hours until he'd served his sentence and could go and join Mabel in Eternity.

Yes of course all ghosts were serving their sentences, he said. Did I really think he'd still be here if he had any choice in the matter? He was serving his sentence and he'd be done a lot quicker if I'd let him get on with it. And yes, of course, he could get up and leave his chair; but why should he? Any time he spent out of it would simply be added on to the end of his sentence, so would I please just leave him alone so that he could do his time and join Mabel as soon as possible.

As he talked about Mabel two big tears rolled down his cheeks and ran off the end of his neatly shaven chin to disappear; presumably into Eternity.

'We aren't allowed to talk about Eternity,' he said

2

when I asked him. 'Otherwise everybody would be committing suicide trying to get there.'

'I'm sure I wouldn't,' I said.

'Ah, but you would if you'd seen it,' he replied longingly. He'd had a little glimpse of it when he was up before the Judge; just enough to make him want to get back there as soon as possible.

'Is there anything I can do to shorten your sentence for you?' I said. 'Would you like me to pray for your soul or something ?'

Mr Chelsea gave me a disgusted look. 'I don't believe in that sort of thing,' he said. 'I'm strictly Church of England.'

I really was getting fed up with Mr Chelsea. He might not have had any bad habits, but he was always there, and there wasn't really room for two of us in that bedsit. I'd saved up for ages for a place of my own; worked overtime, gone without new clothes, virtually lived on beans on toast for months to earn my independence, and now I was having to share accommodation with Mr Chelsea. I'd been so looking forward to my privacy – walking about in my nightie, singing, doing my exercises, whatever I felt like doing - all the things you can't do with a retired civil servant sitting in a chair watching everything you do all the time. And now I'd lost it again.

I thought we'd better establish some house rules.

'You wouldn't ever come into the...err... the WC while I was in there would you?' I said hesitantly.

'Of course I wouldn't come into the lavatory!' he replied testily. 'I'm not a criminal! And even if I was you wouldn't have to worry. I don't have any bodily attributes.'

Well he might not have had any bodily attributes but I had and I didn't feel like parading them in front of Mr Chelsea. There isn't any privacy in a bedsit. I was forced to dress either in my minuscule loo and bash my elbows on the walls, or in my tiny little kitchen and risk knocking my few items of crockery off the draining board; the only place I had where I could keep them.

I tried putting the clothes-horse between Mr Chelsea and the bed and draping the bedspread over it, but I could see him when I sat up to read and I was sure he could see me too. Besides I needed the bedspread on the bed. I couldn't afford to keep the gas fire on all night. I compromised by turning his chair to face the wall.

And if Mr Chelsea hadn't committed a crime why was he serving a sentence? I tried asking him.

'Why are you here Mr Chelsea?

'I'm serving my sentence of course.' He could be very obtuse sometimes.

'Yes, I know you are serving your sentence, but why are you doing it in my chair?'

'I'm serving it in my own armchair,' he said assertively. But he looked uncomfortable. I could see he didn't want to tell me what he'd done.

'Mr Chelsea, if you want me to leave you in peace,

you must tell me why you are here. Otherwise I shall sit on you again and you'll have to leave your chair!' I made a move as though to go and sit on him. After three weeks in Mr Chelsea's company I was beginning to get assertive too.

Mr Chelsea squirmed. 'I did something of which I am ashamed,' he said, 'sitting right here in this chair.'

I looked at that very everyday armchair wondering what terrible thing it would have been possible to do in it.

'I was sitting in my armchair, waiting for the Nine O'Clock News to begin when Mabel called to me from upstairs. She had not been very well and had gone to bed early. I should have known dear Mabel would never have called out unless she really needed me, but I wanted to watch the news so I shouted, 'Just a minute Dear,' and waited till I'd seen the headlines.

'Then I went upstairs and found my poor Mabel dead.'

He cried in real earnest this time. I patted his shoulder sympathetically but my hand went straight through and he didn't seem to notice.

'But surely you weren't condemned to haunt the chair just because you didn't come running immediately: I thought all husbands ignored their wives from time to time!'

He squirmed again. 'It's what I did in it afterwards the Judge didn't like. I was so upset because I hadn't gone straight up to Mabel that I took an overdose of Mabel's sleeping tablets and of course I died. We're not supposed to do that, you see.'

5

Poor Mr Chelsea. I felt so sorry for him. But I really did want my bedsit all to myself. My back ached from trying to watch the television sitting on the floor and I couldn't afford another armchair.

I'd have to find a way to get rid of him, but how? An exorcist? I didn't know any exorcists and I couldn't very well start asking around; if I said I'd seen a ghost people would think I was mad. Perhaps I could find out how to do it myself. I tried looking up exorcism in the library but it seemed to be a very complicated, not to say a dangerous, procedure. Apparently one could end up possessed by worse things than Mr Chelsea. I decided against it and went out for a walk. As I passed the auction house I kicked myself for not having thought of the solution before. I'd put the chair back in the auction! I called in and asked if they could come and collect a chair. Yes of course they could collect a chair. They would be delighted to come and collect a chair. They couldn't have been more willing to collect a chair - until I told them where I lived.

'You mean that brown leather chair I delivered to you last month?'

'Errr...yes. I'm not 'avin' that chair back in 'ere! There's somethink wrong with that chair. I've 'ad it back 'ere three times already. It must 'ave a bad smell or somethink. You keep yer chair to yerself missis!'

I gave up and tried sitting on the kitchen stool to watch television. It was not a success. I contem-plated taking the chair to the tip. But what would happen to it there? Would the council men just chop it up? And what would happen to Mr Chelsea if they did? Would he have to haunt the tip for ever, losing all chance of ever seeing his beloved Mabel again? I couldn't do that to the poor old ghost.

Instead, I took to going out as often as possible to avoid him. I went for long walks. I sat and read in the library. I called in to see my old flat mates. It was one of these who finally gave me the idea of what to do with my ghost.

'They've opened the Manor to visitors,' she said. 'Come with me when I go on Sunday. I don't like going to these places alone. I'm always a bit afraid these old houses might be haunted.'

Well, we went and it wasn't, though I had my suspicions about the lady who showed us round. I'd never seen such a pale, emaciated-looking person and she had a nitty-pritty voice just like Mr Chelsea's. And vague! She was so vague that when someone asked her if the dining table was Tudor she said she didn't know!

'I leave all that sort of thing to my husband,' she said. 'He's the expert. He's always buying things at auction and I never know what's coming till it turns up.'

And no she didn't think they had ever had a ghost. She'd love to have a ghost, she said, it would bring in more visitors and they needed lots more visitors if they were ever going to get the roof repaired.

Well if she wanted a ghost she could jolly well have mine! I could hardly wait to get home.

'Mr Chelsea, I'm going to take you to live in a stately home,' I said.

Mr Chelsea did not look pleased. 'Why can't you just let me stay here and get on with my sentence? All I want is to serve my time and get back to Mabel.' I was beginning to wonder how Mabel had put up with him for so long.

'Because you won't let me sit in my own chair and I can't afford another,' I snapped. 'And stop grumbling. If I wasn't so sorry for you I'd just take the chair to the tip and let them chop it up and then where would you be?'

'Oh don't do that.' His pale little eyes opened wide in horror. 'If they destroy my chair I'll never finish my sentence. Please don't do that to me!'

'Then let me take you to the Manor. They've got plenty of chairs so they won't need to sit on yours, but they do need a ghost to attract more visitors so that they can afford to get the roof repaired. You'll be able to serve out your sentence in elegant surroundings and do some good to others at the same time. Now I'm going to take the chair there and just leave it in the hall, so just you jolly well stay invisible till I've been and gone. I don't want anybody asking awkward questions.'

I put on my painting dungarees, tucked my hair up under a cap, rubbed a bit of dark blue eyeshadow onto my chin and hoped I looked masculine enough to convince the vague lady that I was the auctioneers' delivery boy. Then I loaded the chair into the boot and

8

hoped she wouldn't wonder what had happened to the auctioneers' delivery van.

I didn't deceive her for a moment. 'Oh hello my dear, what a nice old chair! How nice to see them employing girls! I see the van's broken down again!'

The pale thin lady wasn't so vague after all. She turned out to be very shrewd indeed. The following week she had her picture splashed all over the front page of the local paper. 'Ghost Shows Secret Hoard to Lady of Manor,' enthused the headline. The article went on to say how the lady had seen a ghost appear in what she said had been her grandfather's old armchair. When he disappeared again she had searched the chair and found a wad of £20 notes stuffed down the back. She said how happy she would be to see lots of visitors and show them the chair, and maybe the ghost would appear again.

If you could murder a ghost, I would have murdered Mr Chelsea! He knew there was money in that chair and he knew I was flat broke; there isn't much you don't know about a person when you're sharing a bedsit. I could have rented a proper flat and bought myself another armchair for a fraction of the money the lady at the Manor had found. I could even have given Mr Chelsea his own room. But no, the habits of a lifetime prevailed. He just couldn't bring himself to volunteer the information.

I determined to go and give Mr Chelsea a piece of my mind. I paid to go into the Manor again so that I could

9

find him and tell him exactly what I thought of him. The chair was just where I'd left it in the hall.

But there was no Mr Chelsea. The chair was empty. He'd done his time and gone to join Mabel in Eternity.

Next time I tidied up I found a £20 note on the floor, hidden behind the waste-paper basket. I suppose I could have dislodged it when I lifted the chair, but I don't think so. I think Mr Chelsea contrived to put it there. It was just the sort of thing he would do. The miserable old nit-picker probably thought he was repaying his debt to society. It was exactly the price I had paid for the chair.

Balalaika

Maura first saw the balalaika in a junk shop window. It wasn't a nice junk shop, not at all the sort she would normally go into. But it was a beautiful balalaika, its triangular front gaily decorated with flowers. She stopped to take a closer look. The label read £10. That was astonishingly cheap; there must be something wrong with it.

She went into the shop.

'I'd like to look at the balalaika, please.'

'It's a bazouki,' replied the woman, thrusting out her narrow jaw aggressively. 'Nah. It's a manderlin,' contradicted the man, pulling himself out of his chair with a heave of his filthy hands. 'A bargain at ten quid. Nothing wrong with it. 'Ere 'ave a look.'

Maura took hold of the balalaika and turned it over carefully, then tapped her finger gently on the back. There didn't seem to be any cracks. She plucked a string experimentally. It was out of tune of course, but it had quite a nice tone. She'd never played a balalaika – she wasn't sure that she'd ever seen one before, but she was a cellist and she knew a sound instrument when she heard one.

'I'll take it,' she said, hunting through her purse to find the right money. She hadn't enough; only a five-pound note and some coins.

'Will you take eight pounds ninety three pence?'

'Oh go on Bill, let 'er 'ave it. 'Ee owes us enough. Let's get some of it back.'

Maura handed over the money and fled before Bill could change his mind. It was a bargain. She didn't know what a balalaika usually cost but she knew it would be a lot more than ten pounds. She could afford it. They'd asked her to do another shift at the coffee bar tonight and they always paid her straight away. They were always offering her extra shifts, though she didn't usually accept. She had too much college work to do. This was her final year and she'd need the best grades possible if she was to get a place in a good orchestra.

The next problem was how to play the balalaika. She'd had a go already, of course, but didn't really know how to tune it. Next free evening she'd take it into the students' bar and maybe there'd be somebody there who'd know how to play it.

There was the usual crowd in the bar.

'Hello Maura, what've you got there, a bally laika?'

She laughed. 'I bought it in a junk shop. Do you

know anybody who knows how to play it?'

'Horace might, he's studying Russian,' said a bespectacled youth.

Horace didn't, but he thought he'd seen Eric with one. He called across the bar to him. 'Hi Eric. Can you show Maura how to play the balalaika?'

A gangling young man came across the room. 'I used to have one of those. Do you mind if I have a go?'

She nodded and handed it to him. He tuned it, then after a few experimental twangs, settled down to play a Russian folk-melody.

The others clapped. 'Can you play Kalinka?' called one of the girls. Eric launched into the well-known melody and the others joined in, tapping their feet and making up the words if they didn't know them. Some other students came and joined them. Even the barman joined in. Eventually they tired of singing and Eric handed the instrument back to Maura.

'Who's he?' Said one of the girls, pointing to a man hovering on the edge of the group.

Maura turned round to look. Near the door stood an odd looking man with a squarish head and a solemn expression on his face.

'Isn't he a bit old to be a student?' She didn't like the look of him.

'Oh that's Ivan,' said one of the boys from another faculty. 'He's a Russian, over here studying English. We don't see much of him. I think he's got a job or something.'

Maura felt uneasy; the man's eyes seemed to be following her across the room. She went to talk to some other music students at the other end of the bar out of sight of Ivan. When she looked round again he'd moved to where he could see her again.

She didn't say anything to her companions because she didn't want anyone to think she couldn't take care of herself, but when she was ready to leave, she walked in the direction of the ladies room, then veered through the telephone alcove and left by the side door. She usually walked home, but this time she caught a passing bus, having first made sure that Ivan hadn't followed her and seen the bus number.

She did not go into the bar again for some days. She was too busy doing extra shifts in the coffee bar and catching up with her cello practice.

She played her balalaika too. She liked it. It sounded good, now that she'd got used to it, and its pretty floral decoration attracted her. She hated to think what could have happened to it if she hadn't rescued it from that dirty, disorganised little shop. It would have been broken or warped with the damp within a few days. She wondered where it had come from. Perhaps there would be a maker's name inside. She took it over to the window to look at it properly.

'Hello, what's this?' She could see something white inside the sound hole. Gently she inserted her finger. A folded piece of paper moved away at her touch and dropped out of sight inside the instrument.

'Drat!' She shook the balalaika gently and the paper fluttered back within reach, but the slightest touch made it drop away again.

'Blast! I need a piece of wire.'

She didn't have a piece of wire, pieces of wire do not normally live in students' bedsits. They live in dads' garden sheds and her dad's shed was almost a hundred miles away.

'Maybe a twist tie from a food bag will work,' she thought. It didn't.

She took the balalaika to the bar again the next evening. The barman would surely have a piece of wire. He did, and he had that piece of paper out of it in no time at all.

'Gosh look,' said Eric. 'It's covered in Russian writing.'

They all stood around peering at it.

'Atomic secrets?' said one.

'Not nowadays, silly,' said another. 'More like industrial espionage.'

'Anyone know what it says?'

'Ask Horace; he's doing Russian.'

'I'll take it to him. His room's next to mine.' One of the girls picked up the paper.

'Do you mind if I play your balalaika at the concert?' said Eric.

'Of course not. I can't play it well enough myself yet.'

The students held a lunchtime charity concert in one

of the city churches every month and the audience liked to hear unusual instruments. Maura had taken her turn at performing the previous month but she also liked to go along to listen.

She arrived late and sat down quietly near the back. A moment or two later she sensed another person come into the seat behind her. She looked round. It was the Russian. She flinched. The sight of that flat staring face made her feel uneasy again. At the end of the concert she went into the vestry to collect her instrument. She told Eric she'd seen Ivan in the church.

'I don't like him. He has a funny way of looking at people,' she said.

'Then why don't you just slip out of the vestry door and go back through the churchyard?'

She took his advice, but wondered if she'd done the right thing, for out of the corner of her eye she was sure she could see the shabby figure of the Russian walking along the other side of the lane, a little behind her. She turned down an alley and darted into a second-hand bookshop she sometimes visited, then waited till some other people were leaving and went out with them. She stayed with the group until they reached the High Street, when she went into the library.

She had a stint at the coffee bar after college that evening, and when she returned she found Ivan standing on the doorstep.

'Oh please,' he said. 'I must speak with you.'

She froze. She wanted nothing more than to rush inside and get away from him but she didn't. If she opened the door he might push his way in with her and then she might be alone in the house with him.

'Oh please,' he said again. 'Please, I think you have my balalaika.'

Maura breathed out slowly; should she give him it, then rush inside and bang the door? Slowly, she stretched out her hand to give him the instrument.

'Oh no, I do not want to take it from you for I know you must have paid money for it. Those terrible people would not have given it away for nothing.'

Maura began to relax. The man seemed more afraid of her than she was of him. He looked as though life had not treated him well. And if he thought that the filthy couple from the junk shop were terrible, then at least he must have had some standards of decency. She noticed that his hands and nails were clean even though his clothes were shabby.

'I suppose it is yours really,' she said, handing it to him again.

'No, it is not mine. I could not pay my rent – I lost my job, you see. So they took my things and locked me out of the house and now I have nothing.'

Maura looked at Ivan sympathetically. He wasn't just student shabby, he had the real patched and darned shabbiness of genuine poverty. His hair looked as though he'd cut it himself and one of his shoes was split in the front so that she could see his toes poking out of it.

Suddenly she knew he couldn't be a spy, or indeed a criminal of any sort. If he'd been a spy he would have been paid for his services, and if he was a criminal, then surely he could have stolen himself some better clothes and shoes. He stood there shivering in the cold night air and all the while they were talking she could hear his stomach rumbling. Goodness, the man must be starving!

'Are you hungry?' she said. She was beginning to feel sorry for this mysterious man.

'It is nothing. I have been too busy to eat today. But my balalaika, you must let me see it. I have left something in it and I must get it back.'

Maura felt a surge of guilt. Whatever was written on that piece of paper must have been very important to Ivan. She didn't know how she was going to tell him they'd already removed it from the instrument and, were even now, getting it translated.

'Would you like to come in for supper?' She felt an impulse to befriend him. Maura had often been hungry and was usually broke, but she'd never experienced the total poverty that left people with toes hanging out of their shoes.

A longing look passed over Ivan's face. He suppressed it quickly.

'I would like to join you, only if you have enough for yourself,' he said.

18

'I have plenty,' she said. 'I have a job. Do come in. Maybe you can teach me to play the balalaika.'

She handed Ivan the balalaika and unlocked the door, and then led him upstairs to her bedsit. She had planned to have spaghetti bolognese tonight. She could easily do some extra spaghetti and they could share the meat sauce. She washed her hands and began to prepare the meal, leaving Ivan to strum quietly on the balalaika. Really, he was good. He ought to be studying music, not English.

She told him so, as she was grating some cheese for the topping. (She'd intended to have the cheese on toast for breakfast but she reckoned Ivan needed it more.)

'I was a professional musician, but now the State can not any more pay the orchestras. Musicians play for money on every street corner in St Petersburg. I did not want to beg. I had a little money saved so I came here to study English. It is easier to earn a living as a tourist guide than as a musician in Russia now.'

Maura went to the cupboard and took out the birthday cake her mother had given her. She'd intended to make it last a whole month, but she hadn't anything else to offer Ivan. Out of the corner of her eye she could see him trying to see down the hole, into the instrument. She'd have to tell him that she'd already removed the paper.

Someone rapped on the door. 'Telephone for you.'

She went down to the hall to answer it. It was Horace.

'I've translated your secret message for you,' he said. Maura looked up guiltily to make sure Ivan was not listening over the banisters.

'It's just a love poem, very earnest and sentimental. It sounds as though the poet's hopelessly in love with a married lady.'

'Don't tell anybody,' she said. 'I think I know who wrote it and I'd like to give it back to him.'

'OK. I'll let you have it back next time I see you.'

'So that's the big secret,' Maura thought to herself as she returned to the flat. She found Ivan turning down the gas under the spaghetti which was threatening to boil over.

'I'm afraid we found your poem,' she said.

He started guiltily.

'Horace has translated it, but you needn't worry, he won't say anything. Are you very much in love with her?'

'I'm not in love with her at all now.' He looked disgusted with himself. 'When I told her I adored her she laughed at me and called me a silly fool, then I was cured.'

'Then why were you so anxious to get your poem back?'

'Because her husband's the Chief of Police. If he ever found out I had dared to love his wife he'd have me in prison and maybe break up my face, so that no lady would ever look at me again.'

Maura shuddered. 'I'll give you your poem back as

soon as I get it from Horace, then you can burn it. But don't worry, the Russian police can't get you now that you're here.'

Ivan ate his spaghetti, then finished off all of the birthday cake.

'Poor man,' she thought. 'He really does need looking after.'

Then she had an inspiration. She'd get Ivan solvent again and give herself more time for practice at the same time!

'Ivan,' she said. 'Would you like to work in a coffee bar?'

'Can you get me work?'

'They are always wanting me to work more shifts than I have time for. I'd be very grateful if you could do some of them for me.'

Ivan smiled.

She noticed that he had the most wonderful brown eyes.

A Brief Encounter

The rain slopped down the windscreen blotting out the motorway ahead. Oh how she hated this journey; two hundred miles every Friday since Christmas and this time her mother hadn't even recognised her.

A lorry swept past, covering the windscreen with mud. She reached for the wash button hoping there would be enough water to last the journey; she'd forgotten to top it up before she left. A sign "Services 3 miles" loomed out of the murk. She'd stop there and top up. She'd have to ring Janet anyway; the traffic was so slow tonight she was bound to be late picking up Katie.

She turned on the radio to distract herself. 'What is that tune,' she thought as the haunting notes of the oboe filled the air. Then, as the ominous notes of the piano rumbled up from the base, turning into a sharp staccato of dramatic chords, she recognised the Rachmaninov Piano Concerto.

'Of Course! The theme from Brief Encounter.' The music suited her mood and she sang loudly along with it, releasing the tensions built up during the day. She reached the service station and sat in silence in the car park for a few minutes, then switched on her mobile and phoned Janet.

'I'm going to be late home, the traffic's awfully bad tonight. I'm ever so sorry.'

'Don't worry about it. Katie will be all right with us till Bill comes home. She can have her tea with David and Sally.'

'Oh you're wonderful. I don't know what I'd do without you.' She felt a rush of gratitude towards her friend.

'Look, why don't you stay at the services and have a meal and wait till the rush hour's over?' Janet continued. 'I'll ask Bill if he'd like to join us – it's only egg and chips so it'll be easy to cater for one more. It will save you having to cook when you get home.'

'Thanks. I'll do that.'

The cafeteria was bright and busy and she had to queue. The smell of food tempted her and she treated herself to steak and kidney pie and chips. 'I'll have a large glass of apple juice now,' she thought, 'then a big pot of coffee later.'

She took the tray and looked around for somewhere to sit and was just turning towards the only empty space she could see, when a man moved swiftly across her path, knocking the tray sideways and spilling gravy, chips and apple juice all over her skirt.

'Oh I'm so terribly sorry,' he said, his chin dimpling as he smiled. 'Here, do let me take that from you.' He expertly removed the tray and grasped a handful of paper napkins from a dispenser and handed them to her to mop herself.

'Look, there's some space in the alcove over there; go and find yourself a seat and I'll get you another dinner. Steak pie and chips was it? And was that an apple juice?'

'Oh thanks. That's very kind of you.'

She found herself an empty table in the alcove. It was quieter there, with only a faint hum from the motorway traffic. There was a little background music, quiet and soft, mainly classical. She began to relax.

The man returned with a full tray and a profusion of apologies. A little shy at first, she let him do most of the talking. He was a museum curator, he said, and he did a weekly lecture on archaeology at the university. He liked lecturing; young people kept one on one's toes, but they did tire one out!

She laughed. 'Not as much as children,' she said.

'How many do you have?'

'Just Katie. She's six. But what about you?'

'We don't have any. My wife runs a rescue cattery and she says that keeps her busy enough.'

He grinned cheerily, his smile lighting up his dark brown eyes. She liked his smile. He reminded her of a

25

favourite cousin she hadn't seen since he'd gone to Australia. His easy manner made her forget her shyness and she soon found herself telling him about her weekly visits to the hospice.

He expressed sympathy, then they chatted generally till she noticed that the crowds had departed and the cafeteria was nearly empty. She looked at her watch guiltily.

'Goodness! Is that the time? I must be going. Bill will wonder where on earth I've got to.'

'Can we meet again next week? If we set out a little earlier in the morning we could have a quick coffee perhaps?'

Without thinking she agreed. She hummed to herself as she drove the fifty miles home. She didn't know why she'd agreed. It wasn't the sort of thing she usually did, but she knew she was going to enjoy meeting him again. And a brief chat over a cup of coffee couldn't do any harm, could it?

She set off half an hour early the following week. Katie was at school and Bill was at work so nobody would know. She drove into the service area just in time to see him getting out of his car. She blushed. What should she do, speak first or wait for him to see her and come over to greet her?

She needn't have worried. 'Hello,' he called. 'Nice to see you again.' Then before she knew it they were installed in a corner enjoying coffee and cream cakes. The cafeteria was quiet, he was charming and amusing and all too soon it was time to go. They agreed to meet again next week.

The visit to the hospice passed in a whirl. Her mother had had a bad day the day before and was heavily sedated and didn't wake up. She, sitting quietly with her thoughts full of the man she'd just left, was glad of the silence.

She met him again the next week. The tape played Rachmaninov.

'Lovely music,' he said.

She smiled. She felt it was meant to be their tune.

They met again the next week, and the next week and the next. She'd bought a tape of Rachmaninov's Second Piano Concerto to play on the journey, and he said he'd bought one for himself too. Then one day, near to the end of term, he suggested they have a proper date.

'Let's have a day out together. I don't have to go into college next Friday; the students are all out on a dig. Why don't we meet here then drive into town and look at the cathedral? They say there's a nice teashop there. Your mother didn't know you the last couple of times you went so she surely won't miss you just this once. You could always tell the hospice people you had to do something with Katie's school.'

'Oh I don't think I could do that. I couldn't tell a lie to Bill.'

'You don't have to lie. All you have to do is to leave home at the same time and everybody will think you're just going to see your mother as usual. You deserve a day off after all you've been through. Come on, let's do it, it ought to be fun.'

It was fun, and it had been remarkably easy to arrange. Janet assumed she'd pick up Katie as usual, and when she'd rung the hospice to say she had to go to a school meeting nobody seemed to think anything of it.

It was a lovely sunny day, and she felt she would remember it for the rest of her life. They strolled through cool cloisters laughing at the gargoyles, lunched in a pretty teashop, then strolled along the riverbank watching the swans. Apart from themselves the towpath was deserted. Suddenly he reached across and kissed her. It felt like heaven.

'I've wanted to do that for a long time,' he said.

Then without knowing how she got there, she was in his arms. Her head reeled; she could feel his heart beating against her cheek.

A couple approached hand in hand. They moved apart. The other couple smiled at them. They found a bench, and sat down looking at the water. A fisherman settled himself on the opposite bank, set up his rod and switched on his radio. She could hear the Rachmaninov Piano Concerto faintly in the distance.

'He's playing our tune,' she thought as they sat together hand in hand.

The sky began to cloud over and the music changed to a brash military march. She shivered. Suddenly, with a loud hissing and beating of wings, two swans reared up out of the water and started fighting each other. The dream shattered.

'I think we'd better be going, it's getting late,' she said.

'It's been a lovely day, thank you,' he replied.

They walked to the car park in silence. It had been a lovely day, but it had been a mistake. Preoccupied with her guilt, she didn't really listen to what he was saying and when he asked her to meet him for coffee next week she agreed without thinking.

Back at the car her mobile phone was flashing. It was a message from Janet. Katie had been taken ill with neck pains and vomiting and Janet had sent for the doctor. Frantic with anxiety she drove home fast, breaking the speed limits and ignoring angry hoots and flashes from the other motorists. Without bothering to lock the car she raced up Janet's drive and banged on the knocker.

Janet opened the door smiling. 'It's all right, it's not Meningitis,' she said.

'Come in. Katie's asleep in the spare room. The doctor says she's just pulled a muscle and made herself sick with pain. He's given her a mild painkiller and now she's fine. He said to give her a hot water bottle and he's left a bottle of medicine to give her later. I'll go and get it for you.'

Katie looked small and vulnerable against the blue frill of Janet's best bed linen. Her heart lurched as she thought what could have happened while she was away enjoying herself. She felt a surge of gratitude for Janet's cheerful common sense, and wondered how she could possibly have risked losing her friendship by indulging in a silly flirtation. She had an urge to confess all to Janet, but suppressed it; she'd just have to live with her conscience, and serve her right.

Janet came back into the bedroom looking sheepish. 'I'm afraid it's all been my fault,' she said. 'I left the children playing in the garden while I did the ironing. I kept looking out of the window and they seemed to be all right, then Katie started crying and David ran in and said she'd been sick.

'Later, when the doctor said she'd pulled a muscle, I asked David and Jane what they'd been up to and they said they'd seen this video at school about owls. Apparently they can turn their heads right round and look backwards. So the children started playing this silly game seeing how far they could twist each other's heads around.'

'Really, kids!' She smiled to show that she didn't hold Janet responsible in any way.'

'Katie can stay here till she wakes up,' said Janet. 'If you want to go and get Bill's dinner ready I'll ring you when it's time to come and collect her.'

She drove home resolved to give up seeing this man again. Secret romances just didn't fit in with happy family life. She'd keep the next appointment only to tell him they couldn't meet again, then it would all be over and done with.

She spent the next week alternating between guilty and exhilarated, her feelings for her family jostling with the memory of his kisses. When next they met she tried to find words to say they mustn't meet again, but every time she began to say it he headed her off with a smile, a joke or a compliment. When she managed to say it at last it came out in a rush.

'Look, we can't go on meeting like this. I think we ought to make this the last time.'

He smiled and nodded.

'If anybody we knew saw us we could be in trouble,' she continued.

'But nobody has seen us have they? so there's no harm done.' He paused as though thinking.

'Let's make today our last date,' he said. 'Let's make a big thing of it and meet on the way back and have a big dinner to celebrate. There's a notice saying "road works ahead" so we can both phone home to say that there's a lot of hold-ups and we're having dinner on the motorway until the rush hour's over.'

She nodded, relieved that he hadn't made a fuss when she said they would have to part.

'We could have a big celebration dinner in the proper restaurant over the bridge,' he continued. 'They even have non-alcoholic wine so we could pretend we were having the real thing.'

'Oh yes! That sounds lovely. Let's do it.'

She hummed happily to herself as she drove up the motorway towards the hospice. They'd have a lovely time together and then they'd part, and no harm would have been done to anyone.

Her mother was awake when she arrived. She was much more alert today. 'You didn't come last week,' she said.

'I had to go to a school meeting.' The lie tripped readily off her tongue. It's so much easier to tell a falsehood when you've told it once before.

'You promised to show me Katie's school photographs. Did you bring them?'

She flinched with guilt. She'd forgotten about the photographs. She resolved to spend more time with her mother to make up for her negligence.

Her mother couldn't speak for long and soon drifted off to sleep again. She sat holding her mother's hand, thinking about Katie, and about Bill. Bill was boring; she had to admit it. After nearly ten years of marriage, she'd heard all of his stories before. He couldn't bear change of any sort – why, she scarcely dared even try a new recipe! But he loved her and adored little Katie. She couldn't ever do anything to hurt Bill. She'd enjoy her evening out, then be totally faithful to Bill forever afterwards.

The chaplain came in for a quiet word. She liked him. A shy young man with a limp, he knew all his patients and their families and made a point of always being there when he was needed. 'Call me Sam,' he'd said when they first met, and hitherto she always had.

But suddenly without thinking, she heard herself saying, 'Bless me father.'

Sam's eyebrows lifted slightly in surprise, then he raised his hand in blessing. She shut her eyes. 'Bless me father for I have sinned,' she thought wryly as she felt the light breeze of Sam's hand passing before her face. Guilt flooded over her. She longed to confide in Sam, but she couldn't. Her mother might wake up and hear them, and she'd be so sad. She'd always liked Bill.

She'd speak to Sam in private afterwards. Yes, that's what she'd do. She opened her eyes and was about to ask, when a flushed young nurse put her head round the door. Would Sam come quickly to Mr Soper, please?

She took her leave and her mind in turmoil, drove down the motorway to the rendezvous. They met in the car park and strolled across the bridge to the restaurant. A notice on the door said, "Restaurant closed for renovation. Please use the cafeteria on the other side."

He laughed. 'There goes our farewell dinner,' he said.

He paused as though thinking, then he said, 'I say, why don't we go to the motel? We've got a good couple of hours before we need to set off again.'

She felt guilty.

'It would be a lovely way to say farewell.' He looked down at her, smiling tenderly. Her heart leapt.

'Yes, why not?' she said.

They walked across the tarmac in pretended nonchalance. 'I'll get my briefcase. It looks better if you've got some luggage.'

'And I'll get my holdall. It's full of my mother's laundry actually, but nobody'll know.' She laughed shakily.

They signed in and the receptionist gave them a numbered key, and said 'Second left on the upper floor.' She could have sworn she saw the woman smirk.

Inside the bedroom, she looked round her embarrassed. The cold impersonality of the room depressed her. It was a mistake. She shouldn't have come.

To cover her confusion she went over to the window, then drew back in alarm as a girl in chambermaid's uniform came up the steps and went into the room next door. It was Janet's niece! Janet said she'd taken a job but she'd never said where. What if she came into their bedroom and recognised her?

'I can't stay, that girl knows me.' she said, and grabbing her holdall, she fled from the room. Without looking back she ran to her car and drove home as fast as she could.

She must have been mad. What if she'd been caught? What would Bill think if he ever found out?

Of course she didn't want to ruin her marriage, and now that she'd nearly done it she realised just how much Bill meant to her. She prayed he would never find out. And if Janet's niece had recognised her and told her aunt what on earth would Janet think of her?

She reached for the radio to calm her nerves, but she'd left the tape in and the harsh hammering sounds of Rachmaninov's finale rent the air.

'Damn Rachmaninov,' she said, pulling the tape out and throwing it out of the window. The motorist behind honked angrily. She shook herself in annoyance. Having just avoided committing adultery, she was now driving like a lunatic.

The windscreen misted over and she reached for the wipers. Nothing happened. She laughed shakily as she realised that the mistiness was due to her own tears. She brushed them away and took a deep breath, opening the window all the way to let the chilly wind revive her.

Bill was waiting for her when she got home. They'd let him go early tonight, he said. She turned her back and went into the kitchen to make a drink, hoping he wouldn't notice her red-rimmed eyes. She returned when she was calmer, putting a cup of tea down on the table beside him. He didn't seem to see it. Instead he got up and walked into the kitchen and put the kettle on.

He came back and turned on the television, switching from station to station, then turned away and left it again. The sounds of Rachmaninov's music swept into the room and the images of Trevor Howard and Celia Johnson saying goodbye on the railway station filled the screen.

She stood up and turned it off. Brief encounters might

be all right on the screen, but they were too destructive in real life.

Bill paced the room like a caged animal, then came to a halt in front of her.

'There's something I have to say,' he said.

She cringed. Bill knew! Could Janet's niece have seen her after all? Had somebody else seen them; perhaps that day they kissed and cuddled on the riverbank? She strove to collect her thoughts. What should she do; admit to it or deny it?

'Keep calm,' she told herself. 'Play it by ear. Wait and see how much he really knows. Let Bill speak first. Let him have his say then say as little as you can to save the situation.'

Bill ceased his pacing and sat down on the settee opposite. He didn't look at her. 'I have something serious to tell you,' he said. 'I was hoping not to have to tell you while your mother …until your mother…' He paused and swallowed hard. 'Unfortunately, it won't wait any longer.'

He got up and strode around the room again before pausing in front of her.

'I don't know how to say this, but I've got to leave you. The thing is…I'm in love with someone else and she's going to have my baby.'

Dyed in the Wool

I had wanted to be a beautician ever since I can remember, but nobody would let me. I left school, enrolled on the course, passed my exams and came top in most of them, but I couldn't get a job. The problem is that I am ugly and nobody wants an ugly beautician.

My tutor suggested I enrol on the hairdressing course. I came top in hairdressing too but I still couldn't get a job. Apparently nobody wants an ugly hairdresser either. The tutors started saying things like, 'Why don't you study word-processing?'

It was about this time that my Great Aunt Matilda died and left me her house. It was a big old house in the sort of tree-lined street where people like walking their dogs. I moved into the house while deciding what to do with my life.

Great Aunt Matilda had also left me Mac, a nice little white West Highland Terrier. I'd always liked Mac; he was a cheerful little thing who always greeted me with a lot of tail-wagging. A neighbour had been looking after him since my Aunt had been taken ill, so I called on her as soon as possible to arrange to take Mac home with me.

The neighbour looked embarrassed. 'I'm sorry he's so dirty. My daughter Dolly bathed him on Tuesday but he always rolls in the dirt as soon as he's let out again. We just can't keep up with him. You will let her carry on walking him, won't you? It means such a lot to Dolly to know she's good at something.'

I said I'd love to let Dolly help to look after Mac. I liked Dolly, she wasn't very bright, but she had nice manners and was naturally good with animals. She walked several dogs and they'd let her do anything with them, even bath them, and that was what gave me the idea. If I couldn't make people beautiful, I'd make dogs beautiful. I'd open my own beauty parlour – for dogs!

I did all the usual things one has to do to start a business. I worked in a poodle parlour to get some experience while the planning permission was coming through and within a few weeks I was ready to start. Dolly's mother asked if I could give her daughter a job, so I gave Dolly a decent haircut and a smart overall and she held the dogs while I made them beautiful and soon we were making a profit.

The only fly in the ointment was Mac. Between us we simply couldn't keep him clean. As soon as we'd washed him he'd find a patch of mud and roll in it. It wasn't good for business having an off-white Westie walking about the place so one day I decided I'd had enough and I dyed him grey.

'My, he does look nice,' said Dolly and she spent the rest of the week telling everybody how clever I'd been. The customers laughed at first, but we were having a very muddy autumn that year. Soon some of them started to come in asking us to dye their dogs in sensible colours too. My fame spread and I had more business than I could handle.

Mostly I did poodles. I loved handling their soft woolly coats. Customers would show me illustrations of dogs in the colours they wanted and I'd make their dogs look just like the ones in the pictures. I did a few cats (it's quite a challenge making a scruffy old cat look just like a Siamese) and a black and white rabbit with markings that needed to be made even. I even got asked to dye a horse!

I don't know why the man wanted his horse dyed. It was a lovely bright bay and I liked it just as it was, but he said it was a present for his wife and he wanted it dark to match her hair. It wasn't easy doing the horse. A nervous skittering thing, it fidgeted and stamped all the time I was dyeing it and Dolly and the man had difficulty in holding it steady.

It was just after I'd done the horse that the police came. They didn't knock; they just walked in and took a photograph of me dyeing a white cat Burmese brown. Then they took me to the police station and started questioning me about the horse.

'You must have known Sunset Bay was stolen,' they said, 'It's been on the telly and in all the papers.'

'His name's not Sunset Bay, it's Sammy. The man said so.'

The policeman laughed. 'Did he come when you called him then?'

I don't think they believed me.

I'm a real beautician now. The Governor said she'd been trying to bring in beauty therapy for years but the Home Office wouldn't pay for it. She thinks it's good for the girls' self-esteem and it encourages them to go straight. Now she lets me do all the girls' hair and teach them to make up properly. I particularly like doing the ones who are going out because it makes them look nice for their boy friends and it helps them to get jobs.

I'm going out myself next week. The Governor sent for me to tell me.

'We're letting you out early,' she said. 'I know you're not a dyed-in-the-wool criminal, just a girl who's easily led. Why don't you sell the house and move to another part of the country where nobody knows you? You can buy another house and start an honest business from scratch.'

I thought this was a very good idea. Mary and Sue thought it was a good idea too. They're being released with me and we're going into business together. Mary's been rescuing lost dogs and Sue's a sales-lady so we are going to rescue poodles, and when I've made them look nice Sue's going to sell them to good homes. It'll be lovely working with poodles again, but I shall miss being a proper beautician!

For the Love of a Lady

Billy's heart leapt as he approached the supermarket. Today he might see his lady. Oh how he wanted to see her again. The first time he'd seen her she'd smiled at him and he'd lost his heart to her forever.

He loved the supermarket with its bright lights and soft music; the ringing tills and murmuring voices. And there were the smells – oh wonderful smells, apples and beetroot, fresh bread and pastries, smoked ham and cheeses and once, the exciting aroma of fresh coffee, from where somebody had spilt a packet. But it was the smells from the detergent counter that thrilled him the most, because it was right beside the non-biological washing powders that he'd first seen the lady.

She was beautiful. Her fair hair rose smoothly from her blue collar to sweep up into a roll at the back of her head, and her skin glowed like porcelain. Crisp and clean, her striped overall clung to her slender figure and when she moved her arm the stripes twirled like a stick of candy rock. It was her legs however that attracted him the most. Slim, sleek, nylon-covered legs, he'd never seen legs like that before. All the other women he knew wore blue jeans or black leggings. He'd smiled and she'd smiled back, but before she could say anything to him, another customer had stopped and asked her something and she'd turned away.

Those great doors standing open in welcome beckoned him with tantalising glimpses of the goods within. The greens, oranges and golds of the greengrocery department stretched out invitingly before him. Was that the lady there, bending over to arrange some radishes? Alas no, just another shop assistant in the same uniform. She didn't even look at Billy as he passed.

He continued past the long shelves of tins, gaudy with coloured labels, then row upon row of rainbow-hued breakfast cereals. And there was his lady, standing in front of the Weetabix writing something on her clip-board. His heart raced. She'd look round and see him any time now. He searched his mind for something suitable to say but before he could say it she had moved on and disappeared from view round the corner by the sugar bags.

He was in dog-food now, passing quickly through the section, then a quick stop in toiletries for some soap. Alas, no lady in toiletries. Down to cheese next, and there she was! Her clip-board tucked away under her arm she was talking to the man behind the fish counter. Oh hurry, hurry up and finish talking to that man, I can't spin cheese out for much longer!

Another customer approached the lady and she

went away with her. 'Gah,' said Billy.

He went on through frozen pies and pizzas to frozen vegetables; and still no sign of his lady. He turned the corner into ice-cream and oh joy, there she was writing something on her sheets of paper again. Billy approached nervously, wondering if he'd be able to say the right thing to her, but before he could get near enough to speak one of the other women called out to her from the tills and the lady was off again.

He couldn't see her at all now. He'd had to stop for some butter and by the time he'd turned the corner there was no sign of her. Oh dear, he'd nearly finished his shopping and he wouldn't be able to go back. Only one last chance, maybe she'd still be helping at the tills.

He rounded the last corner and there she was, checking an enormous stack of tins, bright with red and gold labels. Unfortunately, she was deep in conversation with a young man and didn't look up as Billy passed. In a moment or two he'd be at the checkout and his chances of attracting her attention, gone for another whole week.

Suddenly he had a bright idea. He'd cause a diversion. He'd knock a tin down onto the floor. That would make her look at him, and even if she was annoyed about it he was pretty sure he could win her round. He'd developed a very winning smile – it usually worked on women – it was worth a risk.

Passing the end of the stack he stretched out a hand and pulled out a tin from the middle of the pile. Suddenly, he was surrounded by tins, falling about him, bouncing and clanging, then rolling crazily around the floor. Startled, the lady looked at Billy. Unfortunately, so did everybody else and Billy found himself at the centre of a circle of staring staff and shoppers. Some of them pointed accusingly, others laughed at him.

'I'm so sorry, I don't know what got into him,' said Billy's mother. 'Eee our Billy.' She blushed red with embarrassment.

Billy wanted to turn around and run, but he couldn't. He was firmly lodged in the trolley seat. An important-looking man strode up. 'What on earth is going on Karen?' he said.

'It's all right, Mr Milburn,' said the lady. 'I'll soon get the tins put back again.'

The man looked sternly at Billy. This was just too much for poor Billy; he burst into tears. His mother, trying to hush him, attempted to move away but the trolley wheels caught in the tins and wouldn't turn.

A big man with blue scars on his face began to pick up tins from the floor. 'I'll help you get straight Flower,' he said to the lady. 'I've nothing else to do these days.' Then with a disapproving glance at Billy, 'Little so an' so's they are nowadays.'

Billy howled again.

The lady laughed. 'We've all been kids ourselves once.'

She put her hand in her pocket and drew out a brightly coloured cardboard tube. Removing the lid, she took out a Smartie and popped it into Billy's mouth.

Billy smiled. The lady smiled back. Oh how he loved the lady!

46

Ghost Train

I heard the train again, as I dozed under the tree in the garden. 'I must find out where the railway line is,' I thought sleepily, before dropping off again.

I had a lot of sleep to catch up on after the events of the last few weeks. First, I'd been made redundant. Then, before I'd had time to get used to the idea that I wasn't any use to anybody any more, my parents were killed in a car crash. I can't describe the sense of loss, the overwhelming grief of knowing that two people you have loved simply aren't there any more. The demands of arranging the funeral and tidying up their affairs would at least give me something to do to occupy the time.

There wasn't really all that much to do, my parents had been meticulous in their affairs; bills were paid, bank statements filed, letters answered promptly; but my father had been a retired clergyman and the church authorities wanted the house cleared quickly for the next incumbent.

It was an old letter to my parents from my grandmother that told me I'd been adopted. There was nothing to say from where; no forms, no official letters, no original birth certificate. Shocked and disorientated, I spent the next few days wandering around the adoption agencies, trying to find out who I was and where I'd come from, but they couldn't help. A lot of records had been destroyed in the war, they said, and of course, I could have been privately adopted.

After one particularly fruitless session, I knew I had to get away, so I got into the car and just drove. Somewhere past Bristol I headed off into the Mendips and wandered around the villages, probably lost but not caring much. It was then that I saw the cottage for sale, and I knew I had to buy it.

I don't really know why I wanted it. It wasn't particularly picturesque, just a labourer's cottage, standing with its twin, about a mile outside the village. The scenery was pleasant, but again, nothing spectacular; just rolling hills, a few farms, lots of sheep, and a garden centre on the other side of the road.

The cottage being empty and the price within my redundancy payment, I bought it outright, gave up my flat and moved down to the West Country. Doing up the cottage and garden would give me something useful to do, I thought, and I soon settled into a routine of gardening when it was fine, decorating when it wasn't and lying out under the tree in the garden when it got too hot; and every time I lay under the tree I heard the train.

I didn't like that train. It was an old-fashioned steam train, puffing and clanking and letting off great hisses of steam, just as I remembered them from my childhood days when I'd cling terrified to my mother's hand, half-expecting the monster to reach out and devour me.

I assumed it must be one of those restored steam trains belonging to an amateur railway society, though I couldn't for the life of me work out what they used for a track, as I'd seen no railway lines in the vicinity. I asked Mr Gurney next door where the railway was.

'There be no railway, not since Dr Beeching closed they down. We'd a nice little station once, you could go to Bristol for the day and the Bristol folks would come down here to picnic on the hill. They had a loading yard there for the quarry stone,' he said, pointing to the garden centre. 'Now there's greenhouses where the goods yard used to be and the booking office is where they takes your money for the plants. You must have been dreaming. There's been no trains hereabouts for more'n thirty years.'

If the train were only a dream then it was a very vivid one. The ground shuddered as it approached and I could smell the soot from the engine. I'd lie there curled up tight, a terrified child again, waiting for that horrible hiss of steam.

Mr Gurney liked talking about the past. 'You ought to prune they bushes,' he said, coming round to lend me his tree loppers and offering to give me a hand with the harder bits. Then, when we'd reduced one particularly

49

large shrub down to size, he showed me the small gate it had been hiding.

'That leads to Lovers Lane,' he said, pointing to a narrow pathway choked with brambles. 'It used to be a short-cut between the village and the station. The lads used to take their girl friends down there for a walk in the evening, and maybe a kiss and a cuddle when nobody was looking. Now you can't get down there for they blackberries and there be no lovers no more. The young men all left when they shut the quarry down.'

The weather grew warmer and I did more and more dreaming beneath the tree. It was always the same dream, the train coming into the station and leaving again, but now, when the train had gone, I heard voices, sounds of young people walking down Lovers Lane, stopping now and then to kiss, or to whisper sweet nothings.

'You've been dreaming again,' said Mr Gurney. 'Nobody's been down Lovers Lane.' He pointed to the brambles. They were as vicious as ever; nobody could possibly have got past them.

As May melted into June the voices became clearer. It was always the same couple, a well-spoken young girl and a man with an American accent.

Mr Gurney didn't like Americans. 'Yanks!' he said spitting into the bushes, 'Over paid, over dressed, over sexed and over here! They with their flashy uniforms and tinned peaches, trying to get away with our girls. They went away for D-Day and never came

50

back. I expect the Jerries got 'em and good riddance!'

'Did one of them get your girlfriend?' I asked, laughing.

'No, Mrs Gurney and me was lovers since we was fourteen, but one of they Yanks got the Vicar's daughter into trouble. Everyone pretended not to notice of course - we thought a lot of our Vicar - but there was no hiding it after a while.'

I shivered. A cloud had come over the sun. Mr Gurney went back to his weeding. He didn't seem to want to talk about the Vicar's daughter.

Next time I heard them, the voices were louder. The lovers were quarrelling; the man shouting, the girl's voice pleading.

'Please Bill, you must, you must,' the girl's voice cracked with tears. 'Oh Bill, why won't you marry me? I'm going to have your baby.'

'I told you why,' the man replied crossly, 'I'm going away to war and I can't marry you. Go to one of those places where they hide you away till you've had it, then get it adopted. Your Dad can fix it. Vicars fix things like that for you girls all the time.'

'But Bill, I don't want to go away and hide,' she wailed, 'I want to marry you, and have our baby, and go back to America with you when the war's over like you promised.'

'Well you can't!' he shouted. 'Do I have to spell it out? I can't marry you!'

'Why, Bill? Why?'

'Because I've got a wife of my own back home! A wife and a new baby I haven't seen yet. I don't care a damn about you and your baby. Go away! Get rid of it! Leave me in peace!'

He stamped off angrily down the lane; the girl left behind sobbing her heart out. 'Bill. Oh Bill!' she kept saying, till she'd cried herself out and I heard her stumbling back to the village.

The next day was hot. I didn't want to go to sleep and hear that train again but I couldn't help it. It was too hot to stay awake.

I heard the train in the distance, then the sound of marching men, the train slowing down, shouted orders, the thuds of goods being loaded, heavy doors slamming, then, as the train pulled out, running footsteps and the anguished cry of a young girl's voice, 'Bill! Oh Bill, won't you even wave goodbye to me?'

I heard the footsteps stumble, then a gasp, a terrified cry, a screeching of metal, an agonised scream and a terrible belching of steam; then silence.

I wanted to get up and run, but I couldn't. Trapped in a nightmare, I could only lie there and listen.

Then suddenly, everything erupted into action; doors opened, booted feet ran hither and thither, men shouted orders and more feet ran hither and thither. A motor vehicle came racing up the hill with its bell clanging. A man's voice shouted, 'Hurry, hurry, I might be able to save the baby.' Then doors slammed shut and the vehicle moved off again, with its loudly clanging bell.

I sat up shivering, despite the hot sun. All was silent, except for the birds. I wanted to scream, to run to the father and mother who were not my father and mother any more, but I had no father and mother, no one to run to but Mr Gurney, placidly weeding his cabbages next door.

'Mr Gurney! Mr Gurney!' I cried, reaching towards him.

'What is it?' He looked startled.

His expression brought me to my senses. It was only a dream. Of course I'd be having nightmares after what I'd gone through in these last few weeks. I couldn't possibly let Mr Gurney know I'd panicked about nothing. I'd talk to him about something else.

'Mr Gurney, what did she look like, the Vicar's daughter?'

'She looked pretty much like her Dad.'

He looked at me quite oddly. 'I've got a photo-graph of the Vicar if you want to see it.'

I nodded and he clumped off indoors and came out again bearing a large framed photograph.

'This be Mrs Gurney and me on our wedding day,' he said proudly. 'And that be the Vicar.' He pointed at the figure standing behind the groom.

I followed his gnarled old finger and looked at the photograph. If you disregarded the clerical uniform and the old-fashioned haircut, the face he was pointing to was the image of my own.

Listen to the Band

'Will you wheel me along to the bandstand dear?' said the old lady shyly. 'I'd love to hear the band again.'

'I can't possibly push you that far against the wind, it's at least half a mile. Besides, they don't play there any more.'

'The band still plays on bank holidays. I can hear them, can't you?'

The girl did not reply; she was too busy looking at some youths with a motorbike and her disco-deadened ears failed to catch the faint strains of music in the distance.

Mrs Wren said nothing as the girl pushed the wheelchair slowly along the promenade. She didn't believe in making a fuss, but she did so much want to hear the band again. She couldn't walk very far these days and though it was very good of the girl to take her out, it was a big disappointment not being able to see the old stand and remember the happy times she'd had there.

She didn't ask again till Whitsun, when Matron said the men from The Guild would be coming to visit. They brought their cars with them and each man took a resident for a ride.

'Can we go past the bandstand please?' she said; but she said it so quietly that the driver didn't hear and took her on a long ride along the cliffs in the other direction instead.

When summer came, Mrs Wren plucked up the courage to ask Matron specially. She'd said that she always used to go to sit by the bandstand on August Bank Holiday Monday and she'd appreciate it very much if Matron could get someone to take her to hear the band playing again. Matron listened courteously, checked the times with the local paper and promised to find someone to take her to listen to the music.

Matron was as good as her word, but unfortunately it wasn't the bandstand Matron thought Mrs Wren had asked to visit. Instead, she arranged for a coach to come to take the residents to Banksand, a stately home with magnificent grounds. The owner opened it to disabled visitors once a year, provided tea and cakes and sandwiches, and hired musicians to play for the visitors. The rest of the residents were delighted. Only Mrs Wren was disappointed.

'Oh dear!' she thought to herself, 'I'm sure everybody's been very kind and I'm glad the others are enjoying themselves, but I'd really rather have gone to listen to the band.' She didn't say so out loud of course, she wouldn't for the world have hurt Matron's feelings.

The next day most of the residents and some of the staff went down with a nasty tummy-bug. Matron wasn't pleased, and said she thought the ham sandwiches served at Banksand must have been to blame. She was very particular about food hygiene in her home and she hoped the doctor didn't think her spotless kitchens could have been the source of the infection.

'Don't worry Matron. Nobody's got it really badly. They'll all be on their feet in a couple of days.' The doctor smiled at her. He liked Matron and it was a joy to visit such a well-run old people's home.

'Just be careful with Mrs Wren, her heart's not been too good lately. When she gets up don't let her walk too far.'

Matron nodded. 'We use the wheelchair if she goes further than the garden, Doctor.'

'She's a splendid old lady. I've known her all my life; she was one of my father's patients before I took over the practice. Not that we saw much of her in surgery in those days; she was always the last one to complain.

'When we were little my father used to take us to hear the band after church every Sunday. Mrs Wren was always there with her boy and girl; we often chatted and I got to know them quite well. My father said she'd had quite a hard life, but you'd never have known it. She was always so cheerful.

'Mrs Wren's husband Bill used to be the band-leader.

Then Bill was killed in the war and Mrs Wren had to put the children in a nursery and go out to work in a factory every day. The hours were long in wartime and the factory girls often had to work overtime, but however busy she was, she always made time to take the children to hear the band every Sunday. She must have scrimped and saved to pay for their music lessons too for she can't have earned very much. She wanted them to be musicians like their father, you see.'

'What happened to the children? She never has any visitors.'

'Mike went off to Australia. He's got his own band now. Marlene followed him out and last I heard she was teaching the piano to diplomats' children in Canberra. Mrs Wren's very proud of them. She was very proud of her husband as well. My father used to say that Bill's band was the best in the county and they were always winning competitions. The best treat you could give Mrs Wren would be to take her to hear the band again. They're playing every Sunday in August and some of the older players might still remember her Bill.'

As she showed the doctor out Matron resolved to go herself to take Mrs Wren to hear the band. Mrs Wren was one of her nicest residents and it would be a pleasure to give her a treat.

Unfortunately, things didn't work out that way. Summer was the busiest time of the year, with staff wanting to go on holiday and temporary residents coming in while their relatives had a break from looking after them. Matron always arranged holiday cover well in advance but, that year, her best locum suddenly announced that she was expecting a baby and another regular holiday helper broke her leg. She felt very bad at not being able to keep her promise but there simply wasn't anybody she could spare for long enough to take Mrs Wren to hear the band.

When things returned to normal and she had time to collect her wits again, Matron saw a notice in the paper saying that the band was going to give a special concert in September; their last performance of the year. She carefully arranged her duty hours to make sure she would be able to leave the house, then told Mrs Wren she was going to take her to the concert on Sunday.

Then half of the staff contracted 'flu and Matron was so busy covering for absentees that she couldn't take any time off at all. She told Mrs Wren how sorry she was and promised faithfully that come what may, she'd see that she got to listen to the band as soon as they started to play again next year.

'Never mind Matron. I know you're very busy. I'll get there somehow. I'll get there in the end.'

The next few days were hectic. With so many staff away sick only the most urgent jobs got done. When Mrs Wren didn't turn up for Sunday tea Matron assumed she must have been resting. Twice she started out to go to bring her downstairs, but each time she was interrupted by a resident needing something urgently.

'I'll get this lot finished then I'll make a fresh tray and take it up to her,' Matron thought to herself as she plodded on wearily. The meal finally ended and she went up to the bedroom to look for Mrs Wren.

Mrs Wren wasn't in her bed. She wasn't in the lounge, the lavatory or the bathroom. Matron checked the lifts, the back stairs, the laundry, the lobby and the garden. She even looked in the store-rooms and the boiler house, though she was certain Mrs Wren wouldn't have gone in there; she was a very sensible old lady and certainly not given to wandering. She was just about to call the staff to an emergency meeting when the phone rang.

'Have you lost an old lady?' a voice enquired.

'Who is this?' Matron's voice was sharp with anxiety.

'It's PC Joe Dale, calling from the bandstand on the promenade. They've just finished the concert and there's an old lady here who doesn't seem to have anyone to take her home.'

'It must be Mrs Wren, we've been looking all over the place for her. I'll be along to collect her directly. Is she all right?'

'She looks in a bad way to me. I've sent for the ambulance.'

Hastily, Matron told one of the helpers to take charge and ran swiftly to her car. Thrusting down her guilty feelings, she tried to concentrate on driving safely through the throng of day-trippers leaving the promenade.

'Oh dear,' she thought, 'I promised to take her to hear the band and now she's made herself ill walking so far, and after Doctor warned me to be careful!'

The bandstand was deserted. The visitors had gone and the chairs put away; all except one.

Mrs Wren sat huddled in the chair. Her eyes were closed, and at first, Matron thought she was already dead. PC Dale hovered anxiously. 'The ambulance will be here any minute now,' he said.

Matron took Mrs Wren's wrist and felt for her pulse. It was thin and thready.

The old lady opened her eyes. 'Hello Matron,' she said. 'You're just in time to hear them play "The Day Thou Gavest Lord is Ended." My Bill always ends with that. That's Bill in the front. Isn't he a handsome fellow?' She began to hum softly to herself.

Matron looked at PC Dale and shook her head. She'd seen death too often not to recognise it when it was coming. She could see the paramedics arriving through the empty bandstand and signalled them to keep away for a moment. They, recognising her uniform, nodded acknowledgement.

Mrs Wren came to the end of the tune, smiled, and waved to the empty bandstand. For a second Matron could have sworn she saw a young man in a 1940's bandmaster's uniform waving back; and yes, he was a handsome fellow!

Manna from Heaven

It was a lovely world. We could scarcely wait for official clearance to go out and explore it. We could see its fresh greenness through the portholes and I had difficulty in restraining some of the more impulsive members of our party from rushing out to savour its delicious dampness.

Our home planet is dry; dry as the dust that settles upon our sensitive skins every time we venture forth upon its surface. The dryness kills, but despite our advanced knowledge and a society civilised enough (now) to abide by its principles, we cannot halt its progress. Our ancestors sinned; they knew the consequences of greed and irresponsibility but they would not listen to the warnings our scientists gave them.

Instead, they wasted precious water in useless recreations and tore out the forests to make way for factories making goods we didn't need, till the earth could no longer trap the moisture and it leaked away into space. Above all, we reproduced. Our species has large families and our forefathers and mothers gave no thought to their impact on other species, or even to their own descendants, as they wallowed in family pride and affection.

At last, our people saw sense, but it was too late to save the way of life nature intended us to enjoy. For generations now, we have lived in caves, away from the merciless sun. Our food is farmed artificially and some of our youngsters have never tasted real vegetation. Our families are restricted; we may have only one child per couple. Even the widowed and remarried may not exceed that quota, however much the new partners long for children of their own.

Our technology is advanced and underground life has enhanced its effectiveness, perhaps because there are few distractions. When two generations ago our leaders suggested putting all our efforts into developing space travel – hitherto just an academic exercise – there was overwhelming support. People gladly gave up precious water to the research establishments and agreed that raw materials could be diverted from the manufacture of what we had hitherto considered to be essential goods. Virtually the whole population helped to develop the technology to colonise other worlds: workers came home from work and did a second shift in the laboratories and even the children helped.

When the first ship was built we were inundated with

applications to join it. At first, once the people with essential skills had been selected, our leaders planned to choose the first colonists by lottery. Then it became obvious during the training programme, that some people just could not live together for months without causing friction, and we realised that we would have to take account of personality traits when choosing the people to populate the new planet.

It was then that I joined the establishment. I am a social psychologist and had gained a lot of experience of helping people to live together in the caves. To be fair, most of our people really do try to co-operate. However, certain character traits – often very desirable character traits such as leadership and innovation – can cause trouble in an enclosed space with restricted social outlets. One has to be careful not to select too many potential leaders!

The character trait I insisted on excluding, however well qualified the person, was a propensity to mysticism. In the early days in the caves, there had been waves of religious mania that led to severe disorder and even deaths among our people. Religious fanaticism can arise at any time but it is particularly likely to occur when people are under prolonged stress, and I can imagine no more stressful a situation than living literally on top of each other sharing a few drops of foul smelling recycled moisture. However much I valued people's rights to believe what they liked I simply could not risk having people claiming a divine right to disobey orders on a space ship.

We selected our new planet carefully. The analysts had detected large quantities of moisture in the air and so far had found no traces of major toxins. Nevertheless, we were careful. As soon as we landed robot sensors analysed and reanalysed soil, air and water samples. All the tests came back positive. This planet really seemed to be the paradise we had hoped it would be.

The captain had great difficulty in persuading the colonists to stay inside the ship while the tests were being made, for despite all my careful screening, a few religious people had managed to get into the crew. Worse, they had smuggled one of their holy books in with them and before we'd got into the orbit of the new planet they had made several converts who believed in every word of what it said.

By the time we'd reached the new planet their leader had started calling it The Promised Land and telling them that God had destined them to inhabit it and we had great difficulty in getting them to stay on board while we were making the essential environmental checks.

Once outside, the clean sweet air seemed to go to their heads. To be honest, it went to all of our heads. To walk where one pleased and to inhale freely, without fear of inhaling our old planet's lethal dry air was a luxury we'd never had before. And the green! Oh the green hills and forests of this new earth. It made our mouths water just to look at such luscious herbage.

The captain allowed only a few of us outside at first and we had a large party of guards on constant alert. Our destination was a forest of great pale green trees, so translucent that we could see the sunlight shining through them. The sun did us no harm. Filtered through moist air and the green of the leaves it refreshed without dehydrating us. We had been told that the plants were not poisonous, but of course they might be unpalatable.

We cast lots for who should be first to taste the leaves, and I was chosen. I had never tasted anything so delightful. I forgot my dignity so far as to give a whoop of glee and say, 'Come on boys, it's delicious,' or some such nonsense, before falling upon that leaf and eating it right down to the ground.

We ate three whole trees between us and made large holes in several more before we were satisfied. Then we remembered our duty to the guards and took over the watch to let them eat.

We saw several creatures in the forest, some also feeding on the emerald foliage around us, but none seemed to take any notice of us. There were great horny creatures walking with jointed legs, not unlike those that once inhabited our own planet, and other large-limbed things that flew through the air above us.

It was when we reported our findings that the religious element among us went berserk. Ignoring the captain's orders and all the rules of safety and caution, they rushed out of the ship singing the praises of some deity or other who had promised them eternal life in a new land. The captain told me to follow them. He knew I couldn't stop them but he hoped I could talk some sense into them when the excitement had had time to die down.

The euphoria spread, and I could do nothing to stop it. It might have been the freedom, or the fresh air, or even some undetected gas in the new planet's atmosphere, but by the time we'd been there for two days, virtually the whole party was mesmerised with the propaganda that this was our promised home and nothing in it could harm us.

The second night, everybody refused to return to the ship and slept out under the stars. Next morning, we found a strange bluish substance upon the ground. It did not seem to be either plant or animal in origin, and bore a slight resemblance to some of the minerals mined on our planet. It smelt delicious.

There was a murmur of wonderment among the people.

'Don't touch it!' I yelled, looking round for the party analyst. I knew the substance wasn't natural; nature abhors regularity.

Nobody heeded me. One of the self-appointed priests was up on a mound praying with his hands raised to heaven. 'The Lord has sent us this miracle food, just as he fed our forefathers in the desert. It is a sign that this is indeed our Promised Land.'

Even the guards were caught up in the general excitement and everybody fell upon the miracle food with cries of pleasure at its wonderful taste.

With difficulty, I managed to control myself. The smell was tantalising and the euphoria infectious. I returned to the ship to take myself out of the way of temptation. When I arrived, nobody else was there; they had all succumbed to the excitement of being free from confinement at last.

I slept fitfully, for I could not forget my anxieties. Perhaps my natural antipathy to religion had biased my reactions, I told myself. But then my common sense would reassert itself and tell me that eating untested food must be dangerous.

I returned to the forest at first light. My uneasiness increased as I approached for there was no sound from my companions, not even snoring. As I came to the place where I had last seen them I could see their bodies lying on the ground, strangely distorted. I raced up to them, opening my first-aid kit as I ran. Not one of them was alive.

I shivered. I was alone in a strange land. I could hear something approaching, something very large; so large that the earth trembled under its feet. I hid under one of the trees, then looked out from between the leaves to see a creature so tall I could scarcely see its head. It walked upon two enormous feet and seemed to have two other appendages carried high above the ground. It bent down to look at my dead companions and emitted a loud bellow.

'Mam! Come and look! There's some funny looking purple and yellow slugs in the lettuce patch.'

'Goodness me, I've never seen anything like those before. Where on earth could they have come from?'

On the Beach

We'd never been to Morecambe. We'd always thought Morecambe a bit of a joke. Carol's grandmother always said she'd never go to Morecambe because her Aunt Mabel had gone there and been swept out to sea by a freak wave and never seen again.

We usually went to somewhere classy for our holiday, Torremolinos, Majorca or Florida or somewhere. Then we got a new baby and I lost my job. I got another but it didn't pay so well so we would have to go without a holiday this summer.

Then one of the typists went to Morecambe. She told us she'd had a marvellous time. 'Look,' she said showing me the brochure, 'here's where we stayed. It's only £19.00 a night B&B, and you get ever such a good a breakfast. Why don't you try it? The landlady's really nice and she loves looking after babies while the mums and dads go out.'

I have to admit I was tempted. The thought of getting

rid of the baby for the evening was overwhelmingly attractive and after all the upheavals we needed a holiday. Maybe Morecambe would be better than nothing, in spite of all those tidal waves that swept great aunties out to sea. I borrowed the brochure for a quick read, and did a quick calculation: we could just about afford it. But how to convince Carol? Then I had a brainwave. Why not let Morecambe sell itself? I phoned the visitors' bureau and asked them to send her a copy and, a few days later, arrived home to find Carol quite taken with it.

I pretended to object a bit, then let her talk me into booking. We decided not to tell anybody where we were going. We told Wayne and Sharon they were going on a mystery holiday and we told everyone else we were going to Torremolinos. We'd been there often enough to sound convincing if we were asked about it afterwards.

As soon as we turned the corner into Morecambe Bay Carol let out a yell of laughter. 'Oh look at that woman!' she said, pointing to a fat lady in a tight red dress standing knee deep in the water. 'She's just like the fat lady they used to have on the comic postcards.'

I slowed down to look, and sure enough there she was, standing facing out to sea, her fat legs braced against the waves, her skirt screwed up around her like a damp red concertina. I laughed so hard I had to stop the car.

The guesthouse wasn't what we were used to but it looked comfortable enough. The landlady was very friendly.

'Oh isn't he a love,' she said holding out her arms for the baby. 'You will let me look after him while you go out won't you?'

'I shouldn't bother if I were you,' said Sharon. 'He's horrible. All he does is yowl.'

'Baby's never cry for me,' she said cuddling him up to her cheek.

We held our breaths in case he started howling again but he didn't, he just smiled and chuckled. The landlady looked after him every single night after that and he never cried once. He'd definitely decided he liked Morecambe.

Wayne and Sharon weren't so sure. They couldn't understand why there wasn't a swimming pool on the premises and a fleet of waiters running around getting people soft drinks with paper umbrellas in. I hoped they weren't going to be difficult. All doubts vanished at breakfast the next morning. The landlady took them to a special table for child guests and introduced them to two other children.

'Hello,' said the girl with a gap-toothed smile, 'I'm Mary and this is Sam my brother and that's my Ma and Da over there.'

Carol winced. She'd always insisted the children call us Mum and Dad. She was very particular about talking properly.

In spite of their accents, Mary's parents were very nice. He was a redundant steelworker from Sheffield and she was doing the night shift at a factory to make ends meet. They were very pleased to meet us and now the children would have somebody to play with.

Carol wasn't so sure. 'They seem very nice but they're not quite our type are they,' she said when we were next alone.

She soon lost her reservations when they offered to take turns at supervising the children on the beach while the adults took a stroll around the town. They showed us the best places to eat cheaply too, so we soon got into the swing of things and began to enjoy ourselves. The weather was fine so we spent a lot of time on the beach and saved even more money. Wayne and Sharon made a lot of friends with the other children and Sam's dad, who knew a lot of the other families from previous years, used to organise games. We asked if the beach was safe and everybody seemed to think it was. None of the regulars had ever heard of a freak wave carrying anyone out to sea.

Every time we went onto the beach we saw the fat lady in the tight red dress, standing quite still staring out to sea. Nobody seemed to know who she was. Sometimes when we were alone at night we had a little giggle about her, but by and large, we forgot about her and got on with enjoying ourselves. We got used to the friendly nosiness of Northerners and were able to relax more, once we'd seen how everybody kept an eye on other people's children on the beach.

Then one day everything went wrong. Carol and I had been for a quick drink in the pub and as we returned to the beach we saw a mass of running men. The lifeguards were reeling out ropes and life belts, the menfolk were all in the water forming a living chain searching the shallows and a speeding boat quartered the waves, its crew leaning over staring into the water. Frantically, we looked around for Wayne and Sharon. We couldn't see them.

'What's happening?' Carol grabbed an old lady.

'Some kids was swept away. There was this great wave...,' she said, but we didn't stay to hear more.

Running down onto the beach we were met by the redundant steelworker's wife, wringing her hands and crying, 'Oh my dear, my dear! I never saw them go into the water. They were digging a hole with Sam and Mary one minute and the next minute they were gone. All I could see was this great wave, and the children being swept out on it. Then they disappeared.' She flung her head into her hands and sobbed wildly.

Carol clung to me and cried, 'I should never have left them, I should never have left them. I should never have come to this place, not after we knew what happened to Great Aunt Mabel!'

I felt a twinge of guilt too, but I couldn't tell her. She must never know I'd sent for the brochure. I couldn't speak. I couldn't look. I was afraid of what I'd see if I did.

Then suddenly, the cries on the beach turned to shouts of excitement. 'Look,' a woman clutched at my arm, 'I think someone's found them.'

I looked out to sea and there, up to her neck in water, was the fat lady in the tight red dress, striding sturdily to shore with a wriggling child under each arm. Hands reached out to take them, then the lifeguard had the children on the sand thumping the water out of them. It didn't take long; a couple of coughs and the pair were sitting up feeling sorry for themselves.

One of the ladies fetched tea from the tea stall; the tea lady refused to take any money for it. Soon everybody was milling around saying how pleased they were that everything was all right, and Carol and I went around thanking everybody for helping.

'Think nothing of it,' said the lifeguard, 'that's what we're here for. Besides it was the lady in red who saved them.'

We'd forgotten about her. We couldn't see her anywhere and nobody seemed to know where she'd gone.

'We've got to find her and thank her,' I said. 'Does anybody know where she lives?'

The lifeguard shook his head, 'I've never seen her before this week.'

'We'll have to try, but it's going to be difficult, we don't even know who she is.'

'Yes we do,' said Sharon. 'She told us. Just as we were going down, and it felt all chokey and horrible, she grabbed us and said, "Its all right, you're quite safe now, Auntie Mabel's got you…"'

One Never Forgets One's First Love

Janet had never seen such a dirty child. She suppressed a wave of revulsion for the whimpering bundle the social worker handed to her. She forced a smile.

'Goodness, where do I begin?'

'Food, of course.' Jo looked strained. 'The Doctor says he doesn't need to go to hospital, he'll be better off with you. All he needs is a good wash and feeding up a bit.'

'What's his name?' Janet led the way into the kitchen.

'I don't know. His mother was too far-gone to tell us. Look, I've got to go and get things moving. Have you got everything?'

'Yes of course.'

'I'll get back to you as soon as we know who she is.' Jo went out to her car and departed.

Janet poured out some cereals and milk. The child stopped whimpering and let her feed him. He looked to be about two years old but he didn't seem to be able to feed himself yet.

The smell revolted her; she'd have to clean the kitchen out when he'd gone to bed. Impatiently she grabbed a handful of tissues, ran them under the tap and tried to wipe the worst of the mess off the boy's face. He wriggled away from her and snivelled.

'Poor little mite,' she thought. 'I don't suppose he's ever felt a loving gesture in his life.' She carried on feeding him till suddenly, as toddlers do, he slumped forward and fell asleep against her arm.

'Hygiene will have to go to pot for once,' she said to herself as she carried his befouled little body to the cot she'd prepared ready for him. Luckily she had plenty of old towels handy.

He was still asleep when Jo phoned to say they still hadn't identified the mother. The girl had only moved into the room a few days previously. That morning her neighbours had felt something was wrong and phoned the police, and when they broke in, they found the baby in a filthy cot and his mother unconscious on the floor with evidence of drug abuse all around her. They'd sent her off in the ambulance and asked Jo to take the child and that was all she could tell Janet at the moment.

She and Jo had worked together for nearly ten years and they understood each other. She smiled as she remembered how they'd first met; Janet the shy would-be foster mother and Jo, the earnest young social worker with her senior hovering in the background. Now Jo was a senior and Janet the experienced foster mother who could be trusted to take any child, however difficult.

This one was going to be difficult. As soon as he was properly awake she sat him in the bath and began to shower the worst of the dirt off him. He cried and tried to wriggle away from her as though he didn't know what bathing was all about. Really, how can people neglect a child, she thought. It must be two days since he was changed. His hair was matted and she thought she saw something crawling underneath it. She sighed, and reached for the special shampoo she always kept handy.

Then suddenly, he looked up, gazing at her with big blue eyes. She caught her breath and choked back a sob. They reminded her so much of Jimmy's eyes. She gave herself a little shake to steady herself. When you lose someone you love you see him everywhere. Strange though that her husband's death should bring back such vivid memories of a love long gone. Maybe it was this child that was making her feel so emotional. These children always did make her feel emotional; however many you've seen you never lose your human feelings.

At first, Jo used to ask her if she wanted to talk about it, but she'd always said no. Then, when she came to know Jo better, she said, 'I'll talk about my feelings if you talk about yours.' Now, whenever they had a particularly distressing case to deal with they both talked about it and it helped to ease the strain.

But she'd never told Jo about Jimmy. Jimmy, her first love, killed in an accident, and little Margaret taken away and adopted. She'd called her baby Margaret though she'd never told anyone. She didn't know what the adoptive parents had called her. That was the way they'd done things in those days; hidden her away in disgrace. Her father shouting and her mother weeping, they'd sent her away to that dreadful home in the country and numb with grief she'd just gone along with what everybody wanted.

They'd moved after that. 'Your father had to change his job because of you,' said her mother accusingly when she returned to a home she'd never seen. 'We've found you a job now so just get on and behave yourself.'

She'd found herself a better job, then a flat of her own, and in the fullness of time she'd met and married Maurice. She'd told Maurice of course, but he just picked her up and hugged her and she knew then that he was the man she wanted to marry. Her parents died in a car crash shortly afterwards and she found she didn't grieve much. And now that Maurice was dead too, there was nobody else who knew about Jimmy.

She'd been so happy with Maurice. They'd had the children, and when they were old enough to understand, the whole family had decided to foster. But despite her happiness, she'd never forgotten Jimmy, and never ceased to grieve for little Margaret. Sometimes she'd wake up crying and feel Maurice's arms go around her and she knew that he knew; though they didn't need to say anything.

She'd had to give up fostering when Maurice was ill. Jo had continued to visit her, and shortly after his death, she'd said, 'Tell me when you're ready.' Soon after that Janet had asked to foster again, and this sad little specimen had arrived.

'I don't think he's been ill-treated,' she said when Jo called later. 'He was very neglected but there weren't any signs of injury on his body. He's got nappy rash of course,' she grinned.

'They usually have,' smiled Jo. 'Nits and nappy-rash. If I had a pound for all the nits I've seen I'd be a millionaire.'

'I'd rather have a pound a nappy,' replied Janet, wrinkling her nose. 'That's the third he's done today.' They both laughed.

Several days passed before Jo could tell her anything more about the boy's mother.

'She appears to be called Sara and she's well known to the Surrey police. She has a long record of petty theft and drug abuse, and now she's taken to robbery with violence. It's to feed her drug habit of course. She's been lying in wait outside post offices on pension day and snatching old ladies' handbags. Then one of the old dears resisted and Sara beat her up quite badly. That's probably why she came to hide up in London. She's been remanded in custody. The old lady's still in hospital, and if she doesn't recover, Sara could be charged with manslaughter.'

'Has she any family?'

'She won't say. Surrey police don't know where she came from.'

'Does she say what the baby's called?'

'Oh yes, sorry, I forgot to tell you. He's called Samson,'

Samson wasn't an easy baby to care for. He cried a lot and wouldn't play with any of the toys Janet gave him. The children were very good with him and tried to keep him entertained; even giving him their favourite old teddy, but he just threw it on the floor.

As there had been no evidence of deliberate abuse, Jo decided that it would be a good thing if Janet took Samson to visit his mother. Janet hated visiting the prison though Samson didn't mind. He seemed to be quite pleased to see his mother, even though she took no notice of him.

Janet didn't like her. A sullen, blotchy-faced girl, she resisted all Janet's attempts to make conversation.

'They're like that when they're coming off the drugs,' the warder said. 'Keep visiting and bring the child. It's often the only thing that keeps them in touch with reality.'

So she kept visiting. Samson could walk and talk a

little now. He'd been more than ready to do both when he came to Janet. All he'd lacked was a little encouragement. He didn't cry so much and though he could still be difficult at times the whole family had become fond of him.

Then, one day when Janet took him to visit the prison, he ran across the room and crawled onto Sara's knee. For the first time, a look of affection spread over her face. A moment or two later it was gone and she looked as dull faced as before. At the next visit however, she picked him up and hugged him. 'Come to your Mam, Samson,' she said.'

Janet felt a twinge of jealousy. Of course she wasn't Samson's mother, she was his foster mother, and she was too experienced to let herself become too fond of somebody else's child. If only he didn't remind her so much of Jimmy. Maybe she should tell Jo about Jimmy, but no, she and Jo had to work together. It wouldn't do.

The girl had been several months in prison now, and at last she was beginning to thaw out a little. Sometimes she asked Janet what Samson had been doing. Janet took some photos of Samson in various activities to show Sara and she seemed really interested.

'Keep coming Janet,' the warder said. 'She's beginning to co-operate with us and I think when she gets out she might keep off the drugs. It's seeing her little boy that does it. She really wants him back.'

Sara's trial date was set for the next month. Jo told

Janet that the old lady had recovered and had left hospital so Sara wouldn't be charged with manslaughter.

'She'll be up on a lesser charge. If she gets a good report she might only get a few months,' she said.

'Will she get Samson back?'

'I don't know. It depends on her being able to convince the court that she'll look after him properly and she won't do that if she hasn't a home to go to.'

Part of Janet wished that Sara would be put away for a good long time so that Samson could stay with her.

'Can't we keep him, Mam?' the children kept saying.

'Now you know we can't. Fostering means that we have to give them back,' she'd always reply, but her heart wasn't in it.

Next time Janet visited, Sara seemed more friendly and ready to chat.

'They've reduced the charges to assault,' she said. 'Maybe I'll be out soon. Do you think they'll let me have Samson back?'

'I don't know.'

Suddenly Janet knew she'd have to level with this girl.

'Look,' she said. 'If you want to keep your son you're going to have to prove you can look after him. If you've got any parents say so, and if they'll agree to have you till you get settled, then you're in with a chance. Have you got any parents?'

'Oh yes, I've got parents.'

'Are they all right? Would they have you back do you think?'

'I don't know. They might. They've taken me back before.' The girl grimaced. 'I'd have to make it up with them of course.'

'Will they be difficult?'

'I don't know.'

Then suddenly she said with a rush, 'They weren't bad parents. We fell out over this boy I was going out with – the one who introduced me to hard drugs – but when he threw me over they took me back.'

'They kept nagging at me to give up the drugs and to get a job so I went off again. Then they took me back when I was on probation, only this time they said I had to go on the drug rehabilitation programme. I couldn't stick it so I left.'

'Do they know about Samson?'

'I don't think so. I never told them.'

'I think you ought to write to them.'

'I'm not apologising.' The girl looked sullen again.

'I don't think you need to. Just tell them that you've got a little boy and ask if they'd like to see him.'

Next visiting day Sara looked happier. 'I've written to my mother,' she said.

'Oh good for you.'

'She might not reply.' The girl lapsed into another of her silences.

The following visit found Sara looking morose again. She'd had no reply from her parents. Janet told her

85

what Samson had been doing at playgroup but she didn't seem interested.

One of the staff came over to speak to Sara. 'We've had a phone call from your parents. They've just arrived back from holiday and will come next visiting day. They said to wish you happy birthday for tomorrow.'

Sara raised her head; her eyes alight with joy. Janet's heart sank like a stone. Tomorrow would be a date she could never forget, for it was the day she'd given birth to the child she'd called Margaret. The daughter she'd given away all those years ago would be twenty tomorrow.

'How old are you Sara?' she managed to say.

'I'll be twenty.'

Janet felt the room swirling around her.

'Miss, Miss come quickly, Janet's fainted.' Sara called to the warder.

Janet came to on the visiting room floor with the prison nurse kneeling beside her. The warder kept the other visitors away while she recovered, then the nurse escorted her to an interview room where she could sit quietly for a while.

'You've really done Sara a lot of good,' said the warder when she came in later. 'It's the first time she's shown any concern for anyone else. There's hope for her yet.'

Sara was released soon afterwards. The court sentenced her to six months, but she'd already served that on remand. She went to live with her parents and visited Samson at Janet's house every weekend. Samson looked forward to seeing her and would climb up onto the window-sill to look out for her.

'I'm pleased with the way Sara's progressing,' Jo said to Janet. 'But I'm not sure she'll stay with her parents. The relationship's a bit strained. She's adopted, by the way.'

'Does she know?'

'No, they never told her. I think they were wrong, but this isn't the time to put it right. She's unstable enough to start fantasising about her real mother and go looking for her and then she might be disappointed. And just imagine the trouble she could cause if she turned up on some unsuspecting woman's doorstep. Goodness, it could unstabilise her whole life.'

Janet knew then, that she would be prepared to let Sara unstablise her whole life if she could have Samson too. She had the children to remember her husband by, but Samson was all she had left of Jimmy.

Sara would be awkward, of course, but she knew she could handle her. An experienced foster mother could handle anything. Her adoptive parents hadn't succeeded with her. And didn't she come confiding in Janet whenever she fell out with them? They had failed her little Margaret: she should never have let her go.

Janet tossed and turned in bed that night, wrestling with her thoughts. Should she tell Sara who she really was and claim back her daughter and grandchild?

Then she'd think of the other couple. They'd given Sara a good home. She'd let them down time after time yet they'd always taken her back. They'd used up all of their savings to hire the best lawyers to defend her. They'd shown their love for her in every way they could. She was their daughter too.

Maybe she should discuss it with Jo. Jo was trained to advise people. If she'd had Jo to advise her when she was sixteen maybe she'd never have given her baby up in the first place. She'd have made her own decision and stuck to it.

Suddenly, she knew that she'd got to make her own decision now. Should she tell Sara or shouldn't she? Only she could decide. She'd let other people make her decisions all those years ago; now she'd make them for herself.

Her opportunity came at the weekend. When Sara said she didn't think she could stick her dad's nagging any more and she felt like running away again, Janet decided.

'Nonsense Sara,' she said with a smile. 'If you could cope with prison you can cope with anything – even with your dad. Look, why don't you just ask Jo to have a word with him? He'll take more notice of her than he will of you.'

Sara wasn't sure, but she promised to try.

Next time Jo called she told Janet she thought that the time had come for Samson to go back to his mother.

'I knew she was ready when she asked me to help her

get on better with her dad. If she's started to take responsibility for that relationship then I think she's ready to take responsibility for her child as well.'

Janet's heart gave a lurch. She'd have to give up Samson now. She'd miss him terribly – they'd all miss him. But she knew she'd done the right thing this time. She'd made her decision and she'd made it herself. She felt she'd taken charge of her own life at last.

Jo called to see her after Samson had gone.

'You'll be pleased to know that Samson's doing well with Sara. Her parents are thrilled with him and her father's so taken with him he's forgetting to nag.'

Janet made a pot of coffee and put some of her home-made biscuits on a plate, then settled down into a chair opposite the social worker.

'Jo,' she said, 'there's something I'd like to tell you.'

The Cat who Climbed Chimneys

Mackerel had a propensity for climbing chimneys. To be fair, old Mrs Lavender didn't know this when she asked the Cat Welfare Society to find a new home for him. She'd had a nice modern flat with central heating so of course it didn't have any chimneys. When she'd taken ill and had to go and live with her daughter, who didn't want a cat, she had absolutely no idea what she was unleashing on the village.

Mackerel was a most attractive cat. 'We'll have no difficulty finding somebody to adopt him,' said the welfare officer as Mackerel climbed onto her knee and rubbed his face against hers. 'He's got a lovely temperament. What beautiful markings he's got.'

'Yes, that's where he got his name; he's a mackerel spotted tabby.'

'Does he like mackerel?'

'Oh yes, he loves fish. He's very good though, he'll eat almost anything you give him.'

'Has he got any bad points?'

'Oh no. He's a very good cat. He's ever so clean and quiet. I hate having to give him up.' Mrs Lavender's eyes filled with tears.

Mrs Snippet patted her hand sympathetically. 'I'm sure he hasn't got any bad habits. I just meant is there anything I ought to know to make sure I don't send him anywhere he won't fit in? Some cats don't like children, for example.'

'Mackerel loves children. He's always running out to play with them.'

'Does he get on with other animals?'

'Oh yes. He never fights. He doesn't even catch birds.'

Mrs Snippet was beginning to think that Mackerel sounded too good to be true. In her experience all cats had something wrong with them. She tried another ploy.

'Why doesn't your daughter like cats?'

'She loves cats but she gets Asthma.'

Mackerel really seemed to be the perfect cat. Clean, quiet, affectionate and well behaved; easy to feed and uninterested in catching birds, he went straight to the top of the adoptions list.

The Vicar was the obvious choice. A sad and lonely bachelor, he lived by himself in an austere Victorian mansion. His mother, who had kept house for him, had recently died. He approached Cat Welfare tentatively; did they think he ought to have a cat, he said?

Of course they thought he ought to have a cat. The Reverend Septimus Saintsbury had a nice big house and garden all to himself, and although everybody knew that vicars were badly paid, he could surely afford to feed one cat. Mrs Snippet took Mackerel to the vicarage the next day. He jumped straight out of the basket and onto Mr Saintsbury's knee and sat there purring loudly. The vicar loved him.

'Oh he's lovely. What's his name? Please do let me have him.'

Mackerel settled into the vicarage at once. He shared the vicar's meals, he shared his bed and he supervised him in the bath; making sure he washed behind his ears properly and helping him with that difficult bit in the middle of the back. Mr Saintsbury had never been so happy since his mother died.

He was a good man. He performed his duties meticulously. He never told lies, cheated at cards or shouted at the children. He never even gave boring sermons from the pulpit. He was almost a saint.

But not quite; the Reverend Septimus Saintsbury had a secret vice. He possessed a rude book and he read it every night!

It was only a magazine, and a very old one at that. He'd confiscated it from a choirboy, intending to put it in the boiler after Evensong, but he'd never got round to it. It was the picture on page three that led to his downfall. It was a terrible picture; so terrible that Mr Saintsbury really couldn't help looking at it. It showed a lady – a rather pretty lady actually – and she had no clothes on!

Mr Saintsbury usually kept his wicked secret in the bedroom, tucked out of sight beneath his pillow where he could reach it easily if he couldn't get off to sleep. But now Mackerel shared his bed he felt too embarrassed to read it in front of him, so he took it downstairs and locked it in the desk in his study.

Mackerel had to be kept out of the study because that was where the vicar wrote his sermons. It is very difficult to think of something suitable to preach about when you've a large cat sitting in your in-tray, tempting you to play football with pieces of rolled up paper. 'Stay in the living room, Puss,' he'd say, giving Mackerel a pat on the head as he went to prepare his weekly homily. Mr Saintsbury always put duty first.

One summer evening, the Vicar had just finished preparing a sermon on the wiles of the Devil. He believed wholeheartedly in the Devil. It was the Devil who tempted men to deviousness and destruction. And surely Beelzebub himself must have spawned the bullies and bellowers, wife-beaters and baby-batterers that so disgraced his parish. Well, the Prince of Darkness wouldn't have a leg to stand on by the time Mr Saintsbury had finished with him. This was going to be his best sermon yet.

His duty done, he could now indulge in a little pleasure. With a guilty thrill, he took the little key from the chain around his neck, unlocked the drawer, drew out the battered magazine and looked at the picture of the naked lady.

Mackerel couldn't understand why his best friend didn't want to play with him. He was bored on his own. He'd played with his little ball with the bell in it and batted his toy mouse until it squeaked. Now he wanted to go string twiddling with Mr Saintsbury.

Maybe he'd better go and look for him. Unfortunately the door was closed. The only way out of the room was up the chimney. Mackerel had a good sense of direction. Could he reach the study via the chimneys? He sat on the hearthrug with his head on one side, staring inside the flue.

Yes, easy, he thought. Lots of nice brickwork to climb up on.' He reached out a paw and stretched upwards, clinging experimentally to the brick. He pulled up with his other paw, then his back legs and soon he was climbing steadily up into the chimney. The chimney branched, but he knew which way led to the study.

Steady now, don't come down too fast, he thought, remembering what his mother had taught him about climbing. 'Oops, nasty lump of soot there, quite slippery underfoot. Oh dear, coming down too fast now. Help!

With a devilish screech, a large black object landed on the study hearthrug, showering the room with soot. A strong smell of sulphur filled the air. Septimus looked up in horror. His sins had found him out. The Devil had come for him at last!

Flinging down the shameful volume, he rushed out of the house yelling that the Devil was after him. So the neighbours called PC Plodding, who took him along to the police station on a Place of Safety Order; and the police surgeon arranged for his admission to hospital.

'Oh dear,' said Mrs Snippet. 'He seemed such a nice man. I was sure poor Mackerel would have had a good home with him. I wonder what he did to him to get him so dirty? I'd better clean him up before I ask the Rockinghams if they would like him.

Mrs Rockingham loved Mackerel on sight. 'Oh what a pretty cat,' she said. 'He's just the thing I want for the children. We're going to adopt, you know. Sally and Tommy have been with us for six months now and they've really settled down. Mrs Filey's coming here next week to give us a final check then, if all's well, they'll really be ours.'

Mackerel adored the Rockingham family. He played football with Tommy and let little Sally pick him up and carry him around for hours. He purred enthusiastically around Mr Rockingham's legs every time he came home from work and he lay on Mrs Rockingham's knee whenever she found time to sit down for a moment.

He didn't get around to exploring the chimneys for a while; he was much too busy keeping the Rockinghams entertained. Then a day came when Mrs Rockingham cleaned the house from top to bottom, even though it wasn't dirty, then washed and changed the children even though they didn't need it. Mr Rockingham came home early from work and changed immediately into his Sunday suit. Nobody seemed to have time to play with Mackerel today so he decided to take a look at the living room chimney.

'Where's Mackwell?' said Sally a little while later. 'I want Mackwell.'

'I want Mackerel too,' said Tommy. 'Mackerel! Where are you Mackerel?'

Mackerel, hearing his name, came down at once and leapt into little Sally's arms. Then he went across to Tommy and gave him a big a cuddle too; he didn't believe in having favourites.

Mrs Rockingham had gone to open the door to Mrs Filey. 'Do come in,' she said. 'The children are waiting for you in the living room.'

Three soot-covered objects rushed forward to greet the social worker. She was nice; they liked her. Sally gave her a kiss and Tommy gave her a hug. Mackerel, not to be outdone, rubbed himself all over her legs. It was a pity she'd brought the Director of Social Services with her, for Mackerel, always diplomatic, felt he ought to make the Director welcome too.

It was Mr Dultery's last visit of the day and he'd arranged to go to dinner with the other chief officers. Now he'd have to ring up and cancel. Drat the

Rockinghams. Suitable for adoption? Not on your life.

The Cat Welfare Officer couldn't understand why Mr and Mrs Rockingham wanted to return Mackerel. He looked healthy enough, and he'd seemed happy there. She wondered where the children were today. She didn't like to ask because Mr Rockingham looked sad and Mrs Rockingham was crying. Perhaps there'd been a death in the family. It didn't do to be too intrusive at such times. She'd take Mackerel away and say nothing. She'd just had another request for a cat.

Miss Chalkwell said she would love to have Mackerel. She'd been so lonely since Tabitha died. Mrs Snippet liked Miss Chalkwell. She'd taught her as she'd taught all the other children in the village. She ran a lovely school, tiny and picturesque; with mums helping in the classroom and the dads rallying round whenever it needed a bit of fund-raising. It was Miss Chalkwell's pride and joy.

The only thorn in Miss Chalkwell's flesh was the County Premises Officer. Mr Parker hated that school. He didn't approve of children enjoying their lessons. The Director of Education wanted to close the school for it was far too small to be run economically. An attractive building like that would fetch a lot of money; his friend the property developer had told him so. However the councillors wouldn't agree to closing the school and one of them had a child there. The Director's only hope was to keep sending Mr Parker to try to find something wrong with the place. Mr Parker

tried, (The property developer was his cousin.)
Whenever he passed the school he'd stop off to have a
little snoop. He was slinking happily around the back
premises the day Mackerel decided to go and join Miss
Chalkwell in the classroom.

Nobody took any notice of Mackerel; it was story time
and Miss Chalkwell was reading "The Water Babies" to
an enthralled audience. So having nothing better to do,
Mackerel went up the chimney. Unfortunately, there
was a bird's nest halfway up and Mackerel got his head
stuck in it.

'Help, help!' he yowled.

Nobody noticed. He yowled again, more loudly this
time.

'Miss, there's something up the chimbley,' said little
Billy Blacker. Billy's dad was the chimney sweep and
Billy was going to be a sweep too when he grew up. He
always noticed things about chimneys.

'Go and take a look, Billy,' said Miss Chalkwell.

Billy looked. So did Bobby, Barry and Barny Blacker.
(Little Benjie wasn't old enough to come to school yet.)

'There's something hanging down, Miss.'

'Well give it a tug and see what happens.'

Billy tugged and Mackerel, indignant at having his tail
pulled, scrabbled through the remains of the nest to seek
safety further up the chimney. Billy tried to climb up
after him and so did Bobby, Barry, and Barny.

Mackerel, afraid of having his tail pulled again,
climbed even faster. Might as well get up to the roof

and go out that way, he thought. Hmm, long way down, I'll have to look out for a soft landing. Oh goody, that man'll do. In Mackerel's experience people liked having cats land upon them.

He leapt. Mr Parker yelled. Miss Chalkwell and the children rushed out to see what was happening and I'm afraid some of the children laughed. That did it. Mr Parker was not going to have the village children laughing at him.

Blowing the soot out of his face he bellowed, 'If this is the way you run your school I'll have you closed down. The classroom's filthy and the children are a disgrace.'

He drove off immediately to tell the Director of Education that the school was a health hazard and that it had wild animals living in the chimney.

Miss Chalkwell was cross and shouted at poor Mackerel when he tried to climb back in through the window. He'd been upset and he wanted a cuddle. Miss Chalkwell didn't want a cuddle. She'd just told the big boys to clean up the classroom and the big girls to clean up the little ones, and she wasn't going to have this great big purring pile of soot messing things up again.

'Get out,' she screamed, and threw a book at him.

Mackerel fled. He didn't like having things flung at him. He kept on running till he reached the other end of the village, then seeing a nice-looking house, jumped in through the open window and looked around for somewhere to have a nap.

Mackerel wasn't the only person in need of a nap. The doctor had had a hectic morning too. Everyone going on holiday had dropped into the surgery for spare prescriptions and all their elderly relatives had decided to be ill just to make sure they felt guilty about going on holiday. Dr Hemmeridge came home exhausted, collapsed into his armchair and fell asleep.

Mackerel thought the doctor's chimney looked inviting. It had a nice dark ledge, full of lovely soft soot, ideal for making a bed. He turned round a few times, sending a few litres of soot cascading into the living room, then curled up and fell fast asleep.

When Dr Hemmeridge woke, he noticed there'd been a soot fall, so he rang the sweep and asked him to come and do the chimney. Mr Blacker said he'd just had a cancellation and could come around now.

Mr Blacker pushed his brush up the chimney. 'Hullo, there's an obstruction of some sort,' he said. He gave the brush an extra hard shove, and it shot up the chimney propelling Mackerel out of the chimney pot.

If Mackerel had been wide awake he'd have landed on his feet, but he wasn't wide awake. He fell onto the tiles on his back, then slithered and bounced down all the way to the gutter where he rolled over the edge and would have fallen had he not managed to hang on with one paw. His back feet scrabbled in empty air. He was terrified and howled for help.

Mr Blacker ran out of the house to see what all the noise was about.

'Hang on Puss, I'm coming,' he called, and he ran to his van for the ladder he used for repairing chimney pots.

Mackerel hung on. There wasn't anything else he could do really, until he felt something solid climb up beneath him. Then he let go of the gutter and clung to Mr Blacker's shoulder, licking his neck in gratitude and purring with relief.

Mr Blacker loved it. 'Easy Puss, you're safe now.' He carried Mackerel down and sat him on the wall to have a good look at him.

'Is he yours, Doctor?'

'No, I don't know whose he is.'

'Better ask around then. I'll just hoover him off a bit first,' he said, giving him a quick go over with the Car Vac he used for cleaning inside his van.

Carrying Mackerel in his arms, he went to look for the cat's owner. He wasn't successful. He began at the vicarage, but there was nobody at home. He called on Mrs Rockingham, who took one look at Mackerel and slammed the door in his face. 'Get that thing out of here,' screamed Miss Chalkwell when he came to see her. There was nothing else for it but to take Mackerel home.

Mr Blacker adored cats. Mrs Blacker said they couldn't afford a cat but maybe this time she'd relent. He wasn't worried about Mackerel going up chimneys for he'd put child guards in all of his. He was proud of those child guards; he'd invented them himself.

Mr Blacker had also invented a very fine shower unit to use when coming home from work. It had a door on the outside leading to a lobby, where he left his dirty clothes, a separate cubicle to shower in, then an exit into the clean side with towels, hair drier and a cupboard for his clean clothes. He thought he'd better take the cat in for a shower too before Mrs Blacker saw it.

'Why, I do believe you're a mackerel-spotted tabby,' he said as he scrubbed the soot off Mackerel. 'I've always liked mackerel tabbies. Here, stand still while I dry you – we can't have you meeting the wife if you're soaking wet.' He played the hair drier on Mackerel.

A shining clean Mr Blacker emerged from the shower to embrace his wife.

'Oh no, not another mouth to feed,' she said looking at the cat in his arms.

'It won't make all that much difference, it's only one more.'

'It isn't actually, it's going to be two more.'

'What! Are you really…?' said a delighted Mr Blacker giving her an even bigger hug.

'I think so.'

'Oh wonderful, maybe we'll get a little girl this time. I've always wanted a little girl. She can wear nice dresses and pretty ribbons in her hair.'

Mrs Blacker didn't agree, though she didn't say anything. No daughter of hers was going to simper around in frilly dresses. She'd grow up to be a chimney sweep like her dad or else!

Mrs Blacker was firm about Mackerel. They couldn't afford to feed a cat. The children didn't know he belonged to Miss Chalkwell. As far as they knew he was just a cat that had come into school. Mrs Blacker telephoned the Cat Welfare Society and asked them to call and collect him.

Mrs Snippet said she was getting ready to go on holiday. Could the Blackers possibly look after the cat for a few days till she'd got back? Mrs Blacker said she supposed she could. Mr Blacker and the children were delighted.

Meanwhile, The Reverend Septimus Saintsbury was not responding to treatment. The psychiatrist didn't believe in the Devil and subjected poor Septimus to every treatment in his repertoire. Luckily, the hospital chaplain did believe in the Devil. He'd had a lot to do with devils, both real and imaginary. He'd been a missionary in Africa till his health gave out and they'd given him this nice easy job in the mental hospital.

Septimus liked the chaplain. Father O'Heckerty didn't try to make him lie down on couches and talk about his mother or stuff nasty-tasting pills down his throat. He offered him a beer instead. Septimus, who usually had beer only at Christmas, bared his soul to father O'Heckerty and told him everything.

The chaplain listened carefully. The vicar's experience didn't sound like the demonic demonstrations he was used to. There must be some other explanation. He probed tactfully.

'Are you sure that what you saw couldn't have had a natural explanation, a soot-fall perhaps?'

'Oh no, it shot across the room and made fearful howling noises.'

'Would you mind if we went back to your house and had a look?'

They went back to the vicarage. Nothing had been moved. PC Plodding had just locked up and left everything the way he'd found it. Father O'Heckerty inspected the fireplace carefully.

'Look Septimus,' he said, 'paw prints; cat's paw prints. There never was a Devil. You've had a cat up the chimney.'

Septimus felt a surge of relief. The Devil wasn't coming for him after all. He felt quite euphoric. Then the feeling left him as he remembered the cat.

'Poor Mackerel,' he said. 'I'd forgotten all about him. I hope somebody's been feeding him.'

'Don't worry, Alf Plodding will have taken him to Cat Welfare when he came to lock up. We can go and get him back for you if you like.'

Septimus shuddered. 'Oh no, I couldn't face him now. He might have seen what I was reading. I'd like to know that he's all right, that's all.'

The chaplain promised to find out. Then he picked up the tattered magazine and looked at it. Compared with the stuff some of the patients smuggled into hospital it was pretty tame.

'Best get rid of this as it's had such a bad effect on

you,' he said. 'Let's tear it up and put it in the bin. Now, where do you keep the cleaning things? If I vacuum the carpet you can wash the hearth and we'll soon have this place looking right again.'

Septimus was happier than he had been for weeks. Now that he knew there wasn't a Devil in it, it was lovely to be back in his own vicarage.

'When do you think they'll let me come home?' he said wistfully.

'You can come home any time you like. You're not being detained under the Mental Health Act.'

'Do you think I could stay at home now?'

'I don't see why not. I'll just pop round and tell the doctor you're back.'

Dr Hemmeridge recognised a fellow professional when he saw one and asked Father O'Heckerty to stay to dinner. Mrs Hemmeridge plied the men with wine, and soon they were rocking with laughter as they recounted tales of patients they had known and other things that can only be talked about within the confidentiality of the professional team.

'That reminds me,' said Father O'Heckerty some time later, 'I promised Septimus I'd find out what happened to his cat.'

'I'll go and phone Doris Snippet,' said Mrs Hemmeridge.

She returned a few minutes later. 'Doris says she gave him to the Rockinghams and he seemed well settled. Then they rang up and asked her to take him away. She says she didn't ask why because they looked as though they were upset about something. Then she gave him to Miss Chalkwell.'

'I wonder what's gone wrong at the Rockingham's,' said Dr Hemmeridge. 'They're a lovely young couple. I've known them since they were just bumps in the antenatal clinic. The last time I saw them they were hoping to adopt – I wrote the reference for them. I'll look in on Mrs Rockingham tomorrow.'

A tearful Mrs Rockingham told him the children had been taken away. 'It was the Director who said we weren't suitable. I know Mrs Filey would have listened to our explanation if he'd let her.'

'The Director of Social Services, Ha! I'll settle him!'

Dr Hemmeridge did not like Alfred Dultery. In his opinion he spent far too much council money on juvenile delinquents and not enough on his elderly patients. He decided to go and sort things out.

Dr Hemmeridge knew one or two things about Mr Dultery; the sort of things doctors know about but aren't allowed to mention. Maybe an oblique reference to that little infection that necessitated his sleeping in the spare room for a while would do the trick. An innocuous remark like: 'I hope Mrs Dultery is keeping well,' should be sufficient to persuade the Director to review the Rockingham's case again.

The doctor didn't need to resort to blackmail. The Director was happy to accept his explanation. As long as he had a reason he could put in writing, he said, he could easily get the decision reversed.

'The Rockinghams did me a good turn as it happens. I was going to dinner with some of the other directors. Wasn't it a good job I didn't!'

Dr Hemmeridge didn't agree. The other chief officers had all been caught leaving the restaurant drunk and disorderly and had lost their jobs. If Alf Dultery had been with them he'd have been sacked as well.

The Reverend Septimus Saintbury was coming along well with his rehabilitation. Father O'Heckerty had insisted he accompany him to the Red Lion every Friday night for a pint. Reluctant at first – he wasn't sure he ought to be seen having a pint in a pub with a Papist – he capitulated when the priest said he needed him there to make sure he didn't have too much to drink.

It was nice and warm in the pub and he was surprised to see so many of his parishioners there. Mr Rockingham popped in to let his friends know that the adoption had gone through successfully. Miss Chalkwell, who'd never been in a pub in her life, thought that, as she was going to lose her job, she might as well get drunk. She came just in time to hear Mr Blacker entertaining his friends with the story of Mackerel's adventures in the chimney.

'Why, that's my cat you've got,' she said.

'Do you want him back?'

'I can't have him back. I've just lost my job and the house that goes with it. I don't know where I'm going to live myself, let alone give a proper home to a cat.'

Septimus was fascinated. He had no idea his cat had been up so many chimneys since he'd last seen him. 'Is Mackerel all right?' he asked Mr Blacker timidly.

'Yes, he's fine. We're looking after him till Mrs Snippet returns from holiday. Would you like him back? I suppose he's yours really.'

'No, I don't think so. I couldn't put up with him going up chimneys all the time.'

'He doesn't go up my chimneys,' said Mr Blacker, wiping a rim of froth from his moustache. 'I've got child guards on 'em all and he can't get through them.'

'Chimney guards!' said Mr Rockingham. 'That's just what we need in our house. Little Sally's always trying to get up the chimney since she saw the cat do it.'

Next time Father O'Heckerty saw Dr Hemmeridge he told him Miss Chalkwell had lost her job. The doctor was furious, and demanded to see the Acting Director of Education. The Acting Director had wanted to be the Director of Education for years but he didn't have the right connections, so now that his predecessor had gone, he was having a lovely time reversing all his decisions. He'd be delighted to reinstate Miss Chalkwell, he said. He sent Mr Parker to tell her the following morning.

So Miss Chalkwell kept her job and her home, but though she knew it wasn't his fault, she couldn't quite forgive Mackerel for his bad behaviour. She told Mrs Snippett she'd rather have a lady cat next time.

'Would you be prepared to take an expectant mother?'

'Of course I would. I've always wanted a house full of kittens.'

'Better send for Mr Blacker then, and get some chimney guards put in.'

Though he didn't have a cat anymore, the Reverend Septimus Saintsbury insisted that Mr Blacker fit safety guards in all of his chimneys too. You never knew what might come down an unguarded chimney.

Installing chimney guards earned Mr Blacker more money than he'd ever had before. Now perhaps his wife would let him keep a cat. Alas no, Dr Hemmeridge had just informed her that she was expecting twins. There wouldn't be room for a cat.

By now Mrs Snippet was getting worried about Mackerel's future. He'd had five homes since Easter and if she didn't get him settled soon he might become maladjusted. She was very relieved therefore when a prosperous looking man called and asked if he might adopt a cat. He wanted a boy, he said, nice and affectionate but with a bit of character. He had a modern house with a big garden and could afford to keep Mackerel in the lap of luxury. And no, he didn't have any chimneys.

She forgot to ask the gentleman what he did for a living but she soon found out. Mr Blacker told her he'd seen Mackerel when he went to install a special cat-friendly double-sided shower-unit for a Mr Surridge.

'What does Mr Surridge do for a living?' she said.

'He cleans out septic tanks.'

110

The Fairy Song

I knew they were fairies as soon as I saw them. It wasn't just their beauty, they had a lightness of limb, a sweetness of voice that set them apart from all the other cats and kittens in the rescue centre.

'I've never seen anything like them,' said the welfare officer shaking her head, 'lovely kittens, but well ... fey if you know what I mean.'

I did. My grandmother knew the fairies. She used to put out a bowl of milk for them every night. 'Be kind to the fairies and they will be kind to you,' she used to say, and certainly her cattle never ailed, and she always won prizes with her vegetables.

'Don't forget to curtsey if you see a fairy, she might be the Fairy Queen,' was another of her sayings. She meant real fairies, not those ridiculous winged midgets children read about in story books, but The Other People, The Old Ones, The Fairy Folk from the Hollow Hills; and surely hills come no hollower than the

Mendips, with their clefts and crannies and half-explored caverns.

Of course I couldn't curtsey to a couple of kittens. The welfare officer would have thought I was mad. The Cat Rescue Society is extremely fussy about the suitability of people it allows to adopt their charges.

'Where did they come from?' I asked.

'The shepherd found them at the top of the hill, hiding in a hollow under the roots of that old hawthorn tree.'

I knew that tree. My Grandmother called it the fairy thorn.

'His dog found them. They were cold and half-starved. He reckoned the mother cat must have been killed, for he looked all over for her but didn't find her. He said old Spot would have found her if she'd been lying injured or trapped anywhere. Maybe she was killed on the road and a fox took the carcass.'

I nodded. I'd often seen foxes patrolling the verges at dusk.

'They're blue tabbies,' she added, referring to their colour, as though so pedestrian a term could do justice to those glowing swirls of Mendip mist and moonlight. Their eyes were the colour of ripe hazel buds, and when they paused in their play to inspect me, I could see behind that wide-eyed kittenish gaze, a hint of something much older.

'They're ready for rehoming now,' she said, 'Would you like them?'

112

I nodded. I had no choice. She completed the paperwork and they were mine to take home.

They were very good kittens. They ate, drank, slept and played, and did all the other things kittens do, but with a grace and delicacy that made all other kittens seem thunderous in comparison. I did not give them tinned cat food. It would not have seemed right. They ate chicken and rabbit, and fish and soft cheese; they drank great draughts of milk from my grandmother's bowl, and always, when I had fed them, they sang to thank me.

It was their song that set them so much apart from other cats and kittens; a high sweet trilling sound of which one never tired. Oh they mewed when they were hungry and purred when they were pleased, just like other cats, but the rest of the time they sang; they sang together when they played and they sang to keep each other company when they were apart. They sang in the garden till the neighbours looked over the hedge to see what musical instrument I was playing.

They loved the garden and they were always out in it, sniffing flowers and playing with falling petals. The garden seemed to love them too, for it bloomed well that summer, and sometimes I could have sworn the flowers turned their heads towards them to be sniffed. They loved chasing butterflies. Not like other kittens, all cruelty and sharp claws, but gambolling with them, leaping and twirling in a swirl of grey mist and bright colours.

'I've never seen anything like them,' the cat lady said again when she came on her follow-up visit. She was watching them catch falling rose petals. 'You'd think they knew which petal was about to fall, and I've never heard sounds like they make, it's almost as though they were singing. I'd love to know where they came from.'

She showed me a photograph of a battered old grey cat. 'Can you keep a look out for this one?' she said. 'She got out of the recovery unit and we think she might be trying to make her way back here. A motorist found her injured at the bottom of the hill and took her straight to her own vet in Shepton. When he was sure the cat would live he gave her to us to look after. She shouldn't have been allowed out yet but somehow she managed to escape. I've wondered if she could be your kittens' mother, she's the same colour as they are and was found near where the shepherd found them. She's probably trying to find her way back to them. Please look out for her. She still needs a lot of nursing.'

I promised to look, and when the welfare officer had gone, I walked all the way round the hill and up to the thorn at the top, but saw no cats, grey or otherwise.

Next morning, when it was still dark, I was woken by the sound of singing from outside. I sat bolt upright. Had the kittens got out? They were too young to be allowed out at night. Full of fears of foxes, badgers, stoats and goodness knows what, I scrambled into my dressing gown and ran downstairs. The kittens were safe enough, sitting on the doormat trilling excitedly, and accompanying them from outside came the same song, but in a deeper, richer voice.

I looked out through the window and saw a gaunt grey cat with great patches of fur missing. I opened the door and said, 'Please come in.'

She limped inside and I shut the door, then I found myself looking into the hazel bud eyes of a woman of my own height. Pale, ill and exhausted, and covered in half-healed scars, she was nevertheless the most beautiful woman I had ever seen, and clinging to her skirts were two little girls of such exquisite fairness that it broke one's heart to look at them.

I curtsied deeply. 'Would you care to join us for breakfast Ma'am.' She looked hungry.

'I should like that very much,' she replied in a deep contralto. 'I haven't eaten for three days.'

She must have been starving. Pausing only to tell the children to remember to eat properly and to use their spoons for their cornflakes, she ate every egg in the house and most of the bread. I put the pitcher of milk in front of her and invited her to help herself and she took me literally: I had to drink my coffee black.

'Why do you take the form of cats Ma'am?' I asked, taking advantage of the pause while I cut some more bread.

'Sometimes We need to go about Our business unobserved,' she said curtly, angry at my intrusion. Then more kindly, with a glint of humour. 'Can you imagine the fuss the Social Services would have made if I'd tried to take my children out of care without telling them who I was and where I lived and what I did for a living?'

I nodded humbly. I hadn't thought about the difficulties fairies must have trying to live in the modern world.

She finished her breakfast and stood up. 'Come children, it's time to go home.'

I held out my arms to say goodbye to my little girls, but they had eyes only for their mother. I shut the door behind them, then ran to the window for one last look, but all I saw was a flash of grey fur as they went through the hedge to the path leading up the hill.

I never saw them again. I leave out bowls of milk, but only the hedgehog drinks it. Sometimes, sitting in the garden at dusk watching the pipistrelles fly, I think I hear the fairy song, but when I hold my breath to listen, there is nothing. And sometimes walking on the hill, I feel something soft brushing against my ankles, but when I look, it is only the drifting thistledown.

Materially, I have been well rewarded. I have never felt so well; not a scratch, not a sprain, not a sniffle, and several aches from old injuries seem to have disappeared. My garden blooms as never before. The old apple tree has borne fruit for the first time in years and I won every prize in the flower show.

I foster now for the Cat Rescue Society. The welfare officer says that I am the best fosterer she has, as I will take in any cat or kitten she offers me. I always hope!

She cannot understand why I never want to adopt any of my fosterlings; lovely cats some of them, more than ready to give me their hearts.

But I cannot give them mine. It belongs forever to my fairy children and is no longer mine to give.

The Bear Pit

There is a road that runs through the oldest part of Sheepstone, from the river to the gaol; a narrow, twisting road, overhung by gaunt grey buildings that look as though they have seen more than their fair share of cruelty and misery.

Giles seemed excited by the gloomy atmosphere. He particularly liked the house by the river. 'It must be at least a hundred years old,' he said.

'More like three hundred,' replied Mr Angel, the estate agent.

Joan didn't like the house. It was dark and had a sour musky smell, as though something mean and miserable had lived in it.

'It's just stale air,' said Giles dismissively. 'It'll go when we've opened a few windows.'

'I don't like it. It's got a nasty atmosphere. I'm sure something bad has happened here. What was it

119

originally Mr Angel? It's got three bricked up arches at the front.'

'It used to be the bear pit,' said the agent. 'I may as well tell you now, because all the locals know. Some of them are quite proud of it actually.'

Of course Giles wanted to buy the bear pit. He liked old things and he often said he wished he'd lived in the fifteenth century when men were men and were allowed to do what they wanted.

Joan liked the house even less when she'd heard its history. 'Please don't buy this house, I couldn't live in it. I'd keep thinking about that poor bear.'

'You're being sentimental. Animals don't have feelings,' he said.

'I'm not sentimental. I grew up on a farm,' said Joan crossly. Giles knew perfectly well that she'd grown up on a farm. He'd used the proceeds from the sale of her parents' farm to buy Giles Ray Enterprises – that and the insurance paid out to him on the death of his previous wife.

'Then it must be that class you go to on comparative religion. She believes in reincarnation,' he said, making a snide man-to-man gesture to the estate agent.

'Maybe she thinks she'll come back as a bear or something,'

Mr Angel didn't rise to it. Instead he smiled at Joan and said, 'I don't see why we shouldn't believe in reincarnation. I've always thought that a kindly God might give the wicked another chance, and let the good who've died young come back to enjoy another, happier life.'

He turned to Giles. 'And if Mrs Ray doesn't like it, there's another house at the top of the hill that's about the same age as this one. It's just come on to the market. It's a bit more expensive but I think the owners would be amenable to negotiation.'

Giles liked the other house too, and of course he negotiated. He never spent more money than he had to. He'd bought his business for a pittance from the receivers, and he'd re-hired the workers at skinflint wages. He therefore surprised Joan by insisting on insuring her life as well as his own when he bought the house, even though she wasn't earning anything.

'We'd have been a lot better off if your parents had insured themselves,' was all he'd say when she asked if it was necessary.

Joan didn't really like the new house though she didn't know why. It was clean, light and recently modernised and had quite a nice outlook. She could see the church from one of the windows, and she could hear the sound of the bells on Sundays. Perhaps it was the view of the gaol from the other window that depressed her. Similar to Reading Goal, in age and appearance, Joan thought of Oscar Wilde's lines every time she looked at it. "In Reading gaol by Reading town, There is a pit of shame."

Though it's that house at the other end of the street that's the real pit of shame, she thought when Giles hired it as a temporary store for some badger pelts he'd bought for making rugs.

'They're not English badgers,' he said dismissively, when Joan expressed concern about killing a protected species. 'They're Chinese. The farmers over there have to cull them to protect the crops.'

Joan wasn't reassured. She didn't like to think about the methods the Chinese might use for culling badgers.

She hadn't seen much of Giles recently. Working hard to set up his new factory, he left early and came home late, haggard and blue-chinned. She joined a local history class, mostly for the company. One evening, the lecturer gave a talk on bear-baiting in Sheepstone. He read out an extract from a document in the county archives, which told of the dark and stormy night when the bear broke loose and terrorised the inhabitants.

"The spectators, full of good beer and merriment, failed to hear the sound of torrential rain, till the river overflowed its banks and stove in the door of the bear pit. In the confusion, the bear broke loose and escaped. It swam across the swollen river and headed for the hills, where it preyed upon the sheep and lambs for the rest of the season.

That winter was the coldest in living memory. The farmers brought down from the hills such sheep as they could get into the barns and left the rest to starve. Everything starved upon the hills that winter; everything except the bear, who came into the town and broke down the doors of smokehouses and storerooms till the people themselves were in danger of starvation. Only the bear-master still had victuals for he had no wife and children to feed.

One night, the bear, smelling the bear-master's meat, battered down the door of his house. Then, seeing before him the man who had tormented him, with one massive paw, smote him in the nether regions, and with the other, swept away all of his face so that he could neither see, nor hear, nor stand, nor use his privy parts, nor even call upon the Lord for mercy, but do nought but lie there howling and groaning for three days till the Lord took pity on him."

'Brrr! I'm glad we didn't buy the old bear pit,' said Joan afterwards.

'What house did you buy?' asked the lecturer, handing Joan the map to point to. 'Why, I do believe you're living in the old bear-masters house! Nobody's sure, but most people think that's the one he lived in.'

Joan didn't sleep that night. Giles was working late so she sat up trying to read. She heard a scream. 'Just a fox,' she said firmly to herself as she got up to make a cup of cocoa.

There was a nasty smell in the kitchen, a sour, musky smell that she couldn't identify. And something seemed to be snuffling around just outside the door. 'A badger on the prowl,' she reassured herself. The snuffling turned to a panting, and the panting to a growling. She looked out of the window but she couldn't see anything. Then the church clock struck two and she saw a large shape move out of a patch of shadow and lumber off down the narrow road towards the river.

She didn't tell Giles but she must have looked peaked, for he brought her a cup of tea in bed the next morning.

'Don't bother to get up; I'll get myself out today,' he said.

Joan was grateful, but the tea tasted funny so she didn't drink it. She had to get up anyway, there was a carpenter coming to fit some cupboards in the kitchen.

She felt better when the man arrived, a normal, cheerful, twenty-first century man, with his bum-cleft rising out of his jeans. It didn't seem so terrible therefore when he knocked off a large piece of plaster to expose a great red-brown stain on the wall.

'Someone's been sillying about with paint,' he said cheerfully. 'It's a pity about the plaster though. It'll all have to be stripped and done again now before I can put your cupboards up.'

Giles wasn't pleased when he heard he'd have to pay a plasterer, but he became quite excited when he saw the state of the stone wall underneath; it was scored from floor to ceiling with great scratches, and covered with splashes of brown stain.

'I bet this is where the bear killed the bear-master,' he said gleefully.

Joan must have looked as sick as she felt, because he continued. 'Never mind. I'll take a day off tomorrow and take you out somewhere. We can walk along the top of Cheddar gorge. You can see for miles from up there.'

Joan looked forward to having Giles to herself all day. Unfortunately, she slipped in the shower next morning and sprained her ankle so they couldn't go.

Whether it was the story of the bear or just the effects of loneliness Joan didn't know, but from then on she felt uneasy whenever she was alone in the house. She went out as much as possible and she started to go to church again, but whatever she did she could never shake off her feelings of unease. She begged Giles not to go out at night and leave her. He laughed at her fears of course, but he began to bring his paperwork home instead. He even suggested taking turns at cooking dinner, though she'd have to wait a few days till he'd finished this round of orders.

It was a hot, sultry night, when Giles finally got around to making the meal. Joan's head ached and she couldn't get enough air. She stepped out into the back yard but there was that strange musky smell again, making her sick. She went back indoors, but her eyes kept straying to the patch of new plaster. The whole house made her feel uneasy. She felt ready to choke.

Suddenly, she could bear it no longer. The foul animal smell seemed all around her now. She had to get out of the house. She opened the front door, but the air seemed just as foul outside.

A brief flicker of moonlight penetrated the heavy cloud, showing the church tower looming up against the darkness. Then she knew had to get to the church.

Ignoring her sprained ankle, she ran out of the house

and staggered through the darkness, bumping into fence posts and tripping over doorsteps, terrified that something evil was lurking in the house behind her. She reached the church door and clutched at the handle. It was locked.

'Oh help me, help me!' she cried, as something roared in the street below her. There was more roaring, then a crashing and splintering of wood. Then a long-drawn scream of anguish, that died away to a terrible, sobbing mutter, as though someone were trying to pray for mercy but no longer had lips to plead with.

They found Joan unconscious on the church steps next morning and sent her to hospital where, eventually, she recovered. The policeman who went to inform the next of kin found the mangled corpse of Giles on the floor.

"Death by misadventure" was the verdict. There were poisonous mushrooms in the casserole Giles had prepared. They said he must have poisoned himself by mistake, and in his death throes, mutilated himself with his own cleaver.

Joan knows differently. She sold Giles Ray Enterprises, and taking only the money that had been hers, bought a farm in the high, sweet air of the Mendips. She donated the rest of Giles' money to a charity that works abroad to rescue bears from captivity.

She had to use a different estate agent for the transactions. Mr Angel seemed to have left Sheepstone and nobody could tell her where he had gone.

The Four Poster Bed

Alice had always wanted to sleep in a four-poster bed. She'd seen one with a pretty lady in it on the television when she was little, and she knew then that she would never be happy until she had slept in one too. The first book she ever bought for herself had a four-poster bed on the cover. She'd seen it in the shop window and saved up her pocket money till she could afford to buy it.

It was a lovely book, written by Belinda Graceland. She'd written to Miss Graceland telling her how much she'd enjoyed the book and how she had always wanted to sleep in a four-poster bed. She received a charming letter from Miss Graceland in reply. "Hold onto your dreams and you will surely find your four-poster bed," she'd written. Alice had kept the letter and read and re-read it. It became a sort of talisman for her and she took it out and read it whenever her Mum was cross or she got ticked off at school for not doing her homework properly.

Her family laughed at her ambition. 'What's a four-poster bed got to do with people like us?' her Mum had said. 'It isn't the bed, it's what goes on in it that counts.'

'Silly old thing,' thought Alice. 'Whatever does she know about romance?' She didn't talk about the bed after that, though she often thought about it and it became her guiding light when she was planning her career.

Alice became a secretary when she left school. 'You're bright and sensible, you could become a secretary,' the career mistress had said. 'Why not stay on in the sixth and do the business studies course? And don't forget, secretaries can go anywhere.'

Anywhere could of course include a castle or a stately home and the long-awaited four-poster bed.

All of Alice's friends had stayed on, except Fred, who said he'd had enough of school and wanted to go and work with his dad as a French polisher. Most of the girls wanted to go out with Fred. With his bright blue eyes and shock of black curling hair, Fred was really quite good looking. Alice liked him herself, but though he often asked her, she would never go out with him. She'd never get near that four-poster bed if she became entangled with a French polisher!

Alice became a secretary in the City. She liked the work and got on well with the other staff. It didn't take her long to find out that a lot of city firms had titled people on their boards of directors. Lords and ladies had castles and castles had four-poster beds, didn't they? She began to spend her lunch hours in the City Business Library looking up companies with aristocrats on the board. One of the merchant banks looked particularly promising; it had two sirs, an honourable and a lord, so when she saw them advertising for a secretary, she applied for the job and got it.

She didn't see much of the titled people at first. She soon found out that the non-executive directors didn't come into the building except for board meetings and the Director's secretary took the minutes for those. Old Sir Jasper was always around, of course. He chatted her up once or twice but she didn't take him seriously; everybody knew that he only lived in a flat in Park Lane. She had realised by now that mere sirs were not worth bothering about. Most of them were only baronets whose grandfathers had bought their titles less than a century ago and they didn't have an ancestral pile among the lot of them.

It was in the holiday season that her chance came. Lord Jim's secretary had booked a holiday in Tenerife and Alice was asked to come and look after Lord Jim for a week.

She enjoyed working for Lord Jim, the work was easy and he was very pleasant. So when he asked her if she'd like to go to Brighton with him for the weekend she said she would. She was surprised to be asked, for she'd been under the impression that he was married; but of course she must have been wrong.

She didn't enjoy the weekend much. She'd hoped to see a bit more of Brighton but Lord Jim seemed to want to spend all the time in the hotel. She supposed it was because the staff knew him so well.

When she went into work on Monday morning the receptionist asked her to wait in the foyer because somebody wanted to speak to her. A few minutes later Lord Jim's secretary, newly tanned from her holiday, handed her a month's wages in an envelope and her personal belongings from her desk drawer in a polythene bag.

'The Company has decided it doesn't need your services any more,' was all she would say.

When Alice asked the receptionist if she could go and say goodbye to her friends, she was told she must leave immediately, but when she asked why, the commissionaire took her firmly by the arm and propelled her to the door.

'You will leave immediately,' he kept repeating.

Alice was very shocked and upset. She couldn't think of anything she had done to trigger instant dismissal. She cried a little when she remembered how she thought she'd been friends with the receptionist and commissionaire, who had always given her a cheery greeting and with whom she had often exchanged pleasantries during the lunch break. It took several readings of Miss Graceland's letter to cheer her up again.

Her next job was with a temping agency. When the

manager asked her why she'd left her last job she thought she'd better tell the truth.

The older woman nodded sagely. 'That happens to a lot of girls,' she said. 'I always tell my temps never to get involved with the boss because it doesn't get you anywhere. He gets what he wants then he gets rid of the evidence and you're out on your ear without a reference.'

Warming to the manager's sympathy, Alice told her she'd always had an ambition to sleep in a four-poster bed. The older woman laughed.

'I'll send you along to the museum. They've got plenty of four-poster beds. They come to us every year and it's a real test of a secretary's abilities. If you do well at the museum we'll keep you on.

The museum administration was chaotic and Alice spent most of the week getting the office sorted out. There were three four-poster beds but they were so well guarded by security alarms that she never even got the chance to put her feet up for ten minutes.

She stayed with the agency. It paid well and they sent her to some interesting places. Several companies asked her if she would stay on permanently but she always said no. She was determined to find her four-poster bed. She knew that if she kept on trying she'd finally succeed; Miss Graceland had told her so.

She thought she might be in sight of her target when she was sent to a major shipping company to look after Lord Doubting. She'd looked him up in 'Who's Who' and found him to be the son of a Viscount. They got on well, and he asked her to stay on as his permanent secretary, but by this time, he'd told her that his father had sold the castle years ago and he now lived in the gatehouse. She stayed with him till his new secretary arrived, then regretfully said goodbye. He was a very nice man.

Then one day, when she was working for a large insurance company, she saw Fred again. Unmistakable with his shock of black curls, his tee shirt and jeans stood out a mile among the city suits in the coffee queue.

'What on earth are you doing here?' she asked.

'I'm restoring the Victorian table in the board room.'

She saw a lot of Fred the next few days and he told her that when he had finished this job he was booked to go to a stately home in Essex to do some restoration of their antique furniture. His dad had done a lot of work for Maudsley End, he said, and they treated him really well. They let him take Mum along too and they slept in a four-poster bed.

When Fred asked Alice out, this time she said yes, and in the fullness of time, she got to sleep in the four-poster bed.

That night, she was cured forever of her interest in four-poster beds. The bed itself was a sad disappointment. The base consisted of ropes stretched across a wooden frame and instead of a proper mattress, it had a sort of linen bag stuffed with lumps of goodness-knows-what. The woodwork creaked alarmingly and the whole thing smelt horribly of woodworm killer.

But her Mum had been right after all. It isn't the bed; it's what goes on in it that counts, and except when she rolled across a particularly hard lump in the mattress or the superstructure creaked especially loudly, she forgot about the bed altogether.

Next morning when Fred asked her to marry him she said yes. Fred said he reckoned he could make a four-poster bed for her if she really wanted but she said no. As soon as they'd found a suitable flat they ordered a nice modern bed from the Co-op and slept happily ever after.

Grandmother's Scissors

Susan shivered and blew on her frozen fingers. She'd lost her gloves somewhere and couldn't afford another pair. Maybe someone would give her some for Christmas. She hurried, trying to complete her round as quickly as possible.

At the next house she had to collect a signature for a recorded delivery. The woman asked if she'd like to come in for a quick cuppa out of the cold.

'I'm sorry, we're not allowed to do that,' she said, 'but it was nice of you to ask.'

'Here,' said the woman. 'Have some mince pies. You're a student aren't you? My son's a student and I know they're always hungry.'

Deftly she slid a few pies from the cooling-rack into a paper bag and handed it to Susan.

'Thanks,' she said smiling. The packet felt warm and she wrapped both hands about it gratefully.

Hot pies. She was ravenous. She'd been at the sorting office since half past five in the morning and hadn't had time to stop since. She sat down in the bus shelter devouring them eagerly.

Several householders waved to her as they passed. They liked the smiling girl in the red bobble hat, who always had a cheery greeting. One or two stopped to wish her a happy Christmas and a shy old lady pressed a note into her palm.

Oh good, she thought, I'll get myself an outsize jar of coffee. It's much cheaper that way and it'll do me till half term.

She called at the supermarket on the way home. 'Economy,' she said firmly to herself. 'Just because you've had a tip it doesn't mean you can spend it all at once.' Dutifully, she filled her basket with bread, pasta and potatoes. She chose the cheapest vegetables and a packet of chicken thighs. Then suddenly, a large red notice caught her attention.

"Pensioners Xmas Dinner", it said, and there gleaming lusciously from the chiller cabinet, was a large cellophane-wrapped tray of roast turkey, trimmed with fresh parsley and accompanied by sausage, two kinds of stuffing, duchesse potatoes, baby carrots and cranberry sauce.

'Bother economy,' she said, putting the carton in her basket and adding a miniature Christmas pudding. 'At least I've saved on the coffee.'

The cold wind hit her as she left the supermarket.

'Brr,' she said. 'It's going to snow tonight.' Ice crystals crackled beneath her feet and twirling the carrier bag handles around her wrists she thrust her hands deep into her pockets. She passed several brightly lit shops on her way home. 'I must buy some Christmas presents,' she thought. 'Goodness, I haven't even sent my cards yet. I hope I'll get some more tips tomorrow.'

She reached the house where she had her bedsit, and fumbled in her pocket for the keys. Unfortunately, her numbed hands couldn't cope with this extra manoeuvre. One of her carrier bags slid off her wrist, hitting the ground with an almighty crash.

'Oh no!' she said aghast. There was no mistaking the sound of splintering glass. The precious jar of coffee lay in a heap of brown grains and glistening fragments. Glumly, she swept it up and put it in the bin.

The house was cold and silent. All the other students had gone home for Christmas. 'I won't get depressed,' she said. 'Look, all those cards and parcels on the table are for me. I'll open them over coffee. Oh drat. I've no coffee now. Well never mind, they say you can make a nice drink with Marmite. And at least I can afford the gas fire now I'm working.'

She lit the gas, then with her fingers rapidly warming round a mug of hot liquid, she opened her mail. Her parents had sent a very generous gift voucher for her favourite store. She felt a rush of homesickness as she read her mother's letter. This was her first Christmas away from home. She longed to be with her family but she couldn't afford the train fare.

She untied her parcels expectantly. A pretty night-dress from her aunt? Oh how lovely. Her best friend had sent her a racy novel: she'd enjoy reading that. But what could this be? The small heavy package was addressed in her father's handwriting. She opened it to find her grandmother's scissors.

Susan's eyes filled with tears. She did so miss her grandmother. She'd been a dressmaker, and she had the most wonderful pair of scissors; large and shining with great dragons twirling about the handles. When she was little Susan had been sure the handles were made of gold.

'They're solid brass,' her grandmother had said. 'They belonged to my grandmother and came all the way from China. Her father used to work on the cargo boats and he brought them back for her when she got engaged. He said they'd bring her luck and they did. They've brought me luck too, and when I'm gone, they're to come to you and my good luck with them.'

Susan held the dragons against her cheek, remembering the old lady who'd passed away so suddenly. Gran had made her own good luck by sheer hard work and cheerful attitude.

She laughed as she untied the last parcel. As soon as she saw the rumpled mass of brown paper tied with unmatching bits of knotted string she knew it could only be from Great Aunt Emma. Her great aunt's knitting was a family joke. Every year, some hideous garment made from oddments of wool would be dutifully acknowledged then donated to the dog's home for bedding.

This time Great Aunt Emma had excelled herself. Instead of the usual multi-coloured mess, she'd stuck to one colour and the scarf and gloves she'd made from it were quite evenly knitted.

The gas fire sputtered and went out and as she reached for another coin to restart it, Susan decided she'd wear the scarf and gloves to work and at least she'd stay warm. She tried them on. Ugh, what a hideous colour – pond scum green. Well the scarf wouldn't show underneath her jacket and nobody cared what you wore on your hands. She looked closely at the wool and laughed.

'So that's why it's all one colour, Great Aunt's recycled that dreadful old jumper of hers. When it finally wore out she must have pulled it out and kept the best bits to knit up again.'

Sitting looking at the mantelpiece covered with cards and with a lap full of presents Susan felt very close to her family and friends. But how was she going to return the favours? Her earnings from the Christmas post were firmly earmarked for next term's expenses.

Her father had given her a cheque at the beginning of term. 'If it isn't enough, you will let me know, won't you.'

Well it wasn't enough. Art materials were much

more expensive than she'd realised. But she couldn't ask for more now, because soon after term began her father had lost his job.

'Don't ever let him know that I told you,' her mother had said over the telephone. 'He's terribly ashamed of it. He wouldn't even tell me at first. He writes dozens of letters and goes to lots of interviews, then he comes back even more depressed than ever. Sometimes I just don't know what to do with him. He yelled the place down when Micky asked him what redundant meant, and after what he said to Joanna when she asked him for a leotard she hasn't dared come near him at all.'

So Susan had found herself a job on the Christmas post and written to say she'd not be home for Christmas. She looked at the scissors again. They were very old and quite unusual. Maybe she could sell them. She didn't want to but it would be worth it if she could buy some presents.

'Victorian,' said the man in the antique shop. 'Nothing much, but I'll give you five pounds for them.'

'No thanks,' she said with a sudden spurt of anger. 'If that's all they're worth I'll keep them.'

'Well now maybe we could do something a little more as…'

But Susan didn't wait to hear him. She knew they were worth more and she wasn't going to do business with him if that was his attitude. She'd keep the scissors. Maybe they'd bring her the luck Grandma had promised.

She strode angrily down the street, averting her eyes as she passed the music shop. She couldn't bear the thought of seeing her own guitar in the window. She'd had to sell it last month to pay the rent. She missed her guitar. It had been a present from her father on her eighteenth birthday. 'You're doing so well at your music you deserve a good instrument,' he'd said.

The young man in the shop had been very nice; not at all like the sneering proprietor of the antique shop, and he'd given her four hundred pounds for the guitar.

The wind nearly knocked her over as she turned the corner and she was glad of Great Aunt Emma's scarf and gloves. There was something to be said for recycling after all. Then suddenly, she had her great idea.

'Recycle!' she thought. 'That's how I'll do it. I'll recycle my Christmas cards.' As soon as she got home she took up the scissors and cut the picture from one of her Christmas cards and glued it onto some spare card left over from one of her projects. It looked professional, so she spent the next half-hour cutting and pasting until she had a pile of cards ready to send.

'I can recycle my presents too,' she thought.

Carefully, she smoothed the wrapping paper trimming off any ragged bits, then re-wrapped the pretty nightie to send to her best friend. The racy novel should please her aunt – she liked racy novels. And she could use the gift voucher to buy presents for her family. The store stayed open late in Christmas week. She could post the parcel tomorrow and with luck they'd get it in time for Christmas.

The store was like fairyland. There were coloured lights everywhere and in every alcove, Santas, elves and reindeer nodded and danced among frost- covered fir trees. A friendly girl offered her a free sample of her favourite perfume and a motherly lady dispensed roast chestnuts to everyone who'd made a purchase.

Susan bought a sweater for her father and for her mother, a book by her favourite author. Micky of course had to have the latest computer game. But what about Joanna; did she still like dolls?

'Oh look,' said a child's voice behind her. 'That little girl's wearing my leotard.'

Susan looked up to see where the child was pointing and there, high above the sports display, was a model ballet dancer in a multi-coloured outfit.

'It's the latest style,' said the saleslady. 'All the little girls are wearing them. There's a special offer on this week. They've been so popular we've been able to negotiate a special price. Would you like it gift-wrapped?'

Susan smiled and nodded. The scissors had brought her luck. She'd been able to buy all the Christmas presents she wanted. She went to the cash desk to pay for her parcels.

'You've a little bit left from your voucher,' the cashier said. 'Why not go and have the special shoppers' dinner in the restaurant. We're giving a two pound voucher to everybody who's spent over fifty pounds today so you'll have enough for a real slap-up meal.'

Susan thanked her. 'I'll do that,' she said.

'You're our Christmas post lady, aren't you?' the woman continued. 'Here, have another voucher.' She smiled conspiratorially. 'You'll have spent over a hundred pounds by the time you've finished your dinner, so you're entitled to it. You'll have to use it up this week, but if you don't want anything else you can always pop in for coffee and cake.'

Susan was glad of her hideous green mitts the next morning. The weather had become steadily worse as Christmas approached. She was offered some overtime and she took it. Naturally, she was tired, but she was pleased she'd made more money for next term.

'I'm glad that's over,' she said to herself as she dragged her numb feet up the drive on Christmas Eve. 'It will be nice not to have to get up at five o'clock in the morning.'

As she turned the key in the lock she heard a car door open behind her and a voice said, 'Susan?'

She turned and looked at the tall man standing by the gate.

'Daddy!' She leapt into his arms and gave him an almighty hug. 'What on earth are you doing here?'

'I've come to take you home for Christmas,' he said. 'Aren't you going to ask me in?'

As he looked round her tiny bedsit he felt in his

pocket for his wallet. 'Is there anything you have to pay for before you go home, your rent perhaps?'

Susan shook her head. 'I'm all right Dad, honestly.'

'You can't be all right if you're wearing Great Aunt Emma's horrible knitting,' he said, and suddenly they were both laughing.

'We knew you were short because you had to sell your guitar; you'd never have parted with it otherwise.'

'How did you find out?'

'The man from the music shop rang last week. Your home address was inside the guitar case. When he saw the instrument he knew it was worth much more than the four hundred pounds his son had given you and he wanted to get in touch to give you some more. I told him to hang on to it and I'd buy it back for you. I called in this afternoon and collected it.'

'But Dad, you can't afford it.'

'Oh can't I? Your grandmother left me her house and I've just sold it to the man who's given me my new job. He wants to do it up for his son.'

'But I thought Grandma had a council house.'

'So she did. But she bought it with the insurance money when your grandfather died and never told anyone.

'Hurry up and get your things together,' he continued. 'I want to get on the motorway before it's dark.'

Susan threw a few clothes into a bag and hastily cleared out the fridge.

'What's this?' her father said, holding out the

pensioner's Christmas dinner.'

'My treat for next term,' said Susan, tossing it into the freezer compartment.

She picked up her grandmother's scissors.

'Surely you're not taking those?'

The twin dragons grinned cheekily at Susan as she put the scissors into her travelling bag.

'Oh yes I am,' she said. 'They've brought me luck.'

Barking Mad

Mike looked at the screen in amazement. He'd just seen his own name on the website. It couldn't be true; surely an ordinary chap like him couldn't be on somebody's hit list?

Anyway he didn't hate dogs; he quite liked them. All he'd done was to ask the dog warden to call on a family of squatters whose dogs barked incessantly day and night.

'You did those dogs a good turn,' she said when she called round later. 'They were barking because they were hungry. The rescue centre says you've probably saved their lives.'

And now he found himself targeted for action by an organisation calling itself Guard Dog.

'Case No 45,' he read. 'Complained to the council about barking dogs.' Why number 45: were they all to be eliminated in numerical order? He took a closer look at the other names on the list.

Greenacres Pharmaceuticals came top, accused of using dogs for drug testing. Numbers 2 and 3 had convictions for cruelty. Mike felt a little sick as he read the details, then a surge of indignation at being lumped together with such people.

The rest seemed fairly innocuous. There was a dog show judge who'd accused breeders of putting profit before the dog's wellbeing and a woman rescuer campaigning for reintroduction of the dog licence. The rest were mostly people who'd complained one way or another about other peoples' dogs.

Mike tried to forget about it. There were plenty of lunatics on the web and it was probably all a hoax.

Then a few days later he read in the paper that the police were investigating the death of a prominent dog show judge. The man had died in a car crash after someone had tampered with his brakes. Mike checked the website again and found that the dead man was the same judge that had been condemned by Guard Dog. It might be a coincidence but Mike felt uneasy all the same.

His own name was now at number 39. Greenacres Pharmaceuticals was still at the top – they probably had well protected premises. That left five in between unaccounted for and he didn't like to think what might have happened to them.

He thought he'd better tell the police but they didn't want to know. They had better things to do than check out loony websites, they said. There was nothing for it but to find out what was behind it for himself.

He took a couple of days leave from work, and fitted window locks and better locks on the doors, then he went through the list again to see if the names would give him any inspiration.

They didn't. They seemed to have nothing in common except an alleged hostility to dogs. He tried to telephone a few but it wasn't easy; some had unlisted numbers and others just didn't want to know. Only the woman who wanted to bring back the dog licence believed him. Someone had just pushed lighted rags through her letterbox.

'Fortunately, my floor's tiled so they just went out,' she said.

'Did you tell the police?'

'No I didn't bother. I'm fairly well known for my views on licensing and they aren't popular.'

Mike went out and bought a couple of fire extinguishers and installed smoke alarms. His number now stood at 36.

He tried to ring the next person on the list but only got a strange buzzing noise, so as the man lived only a few miles away he decided to go and see him. The house wasn't easy to find and Mike had to ask a woman for directions. She seemed surprised.

'Didn't you hear,' she said. 'His house was burnt down last night and him with it.'

Mike's blood ran cold. He drove home scarcely able to concentrate on what he was doing and he searched the house thoroughly before sitting down to the strong coffee his shattered nerves craved.

He rang the police again. They told him to go away unless he wanted to be charged with wasting police time.

Mike looked at Guard Dog every day now and his name was rising slowly towards the top of the list. He packed a suitcase and booked in at a guesthouse.

He couldn't find out any more about the other potential victims. None of them lived locally and only a serious incident would have reached the national news. He decided to ring Greenacres Pharmaceuticals. A company that size must have a security officer: perhaps he would know what to do.

The receptionist wasn't helpful.

'I want to speak to the security manager.'

'What is it about'

'I believe you may be at risk.'

'We're not interested in insurance.'

'I'm not selling insurance. I rang to warn you...'

'If that's another threat from the animal rights people I have to inform you that all calls are being monitored and we have a hot line to the police.' She slammed the phone down.

Mike paced the floor in frustration. Guard Dog meant business. Several hundred employees were at risk. He'd have to go and insist on seeing somebody.

Greenacres Pharmaceuticals was set in idyllic countryside. A long low building, blending sympathetically with the landscape, it could have graced the covers of a rural lifestyle magazine. A woman in a flowery dress was walking along the verge with a Scottie dog on a lead. Nothing could have looked more peaceful.

Suddenly, a bird flew up and the Scottie leapt after it, jerking his owner's arm. She tripped and fell heavily.

Mike pulled up. 'Are you all right? Can I help at all?'

She grimaced. 'I'm not sure. I think I've twisted my ankle.'

'Would you like a lift somewhere?'

'My car's about half a mile away, can you take me?'

'Gladly.' Mike opened the car door.

'You don't mind Charlie?' She indicated the dog. 'You're not one of those dog-haters are you?'

Mikes held his breath, frantically seeking the right answer. She might of course be harmless, but he wasn't taking any chances.

'Hello Charlie,' he said. 'Nice to meet you.'

It seemed to be the right thing to say. The lady got into the car and Charlie leapt in and sat bolt upright on her knee.

'He looks as though he's on guard,' Mike said, by way of conversation.

'Oh no. It's I who have to guard him,' she replied. 'His sister was murdered, you know. It was in the paper; didn't you see it?'

Mike shook his head. 'I don't live round here.'

'It was a teenage delinquent. He stole a car and crashed it into a wall. My little Flora was crushed to death.'

Something cold settled in the pit of Mike's stomach. He recognised the story now. It was one of the Guard Dog cases.

'He only got three months,' she continued. 'He should have got more, but he'll get his deserts before long.'

She must be one of them. Her presence near Greenacres Pharmaceuticals was suspicious. Perhaps she was spying out the land. He'd have to follow her, but she mustn't know.

He took her to her car and said goodbye then waited till she was out of sight before driving as fast as he dared in the same direction. He caught sight of her some minutes later, and making sure he didn't get close enough to be recognised, kept her in sight all the way to a village, where she stopped at a house beside the green.

Taking care to park out of sight, he went into the village shop. The assistant seemed happy to talk.

'The lady in the pink house? That's Mrs Brown.'

'My mother knew a Mrs Brown. I wonder if it's the same one. Is she a teacher?'

'I don't think so. She doesn't have a job. She used to be on the bench.'

'That's a nice little dog she has.'

'She used to have two but a teenager in a stolen car

ran off the road and killed the other one. She resigned from the bench over that, she thought his sentence wasn't long enough.'

'Surely it would have been an accident; people don't deliberately kill dogs.'

'This lad certainly didn't. He was really cut up about it. It was just a teenage prank; he didn't mean to do any harm.'

Mike nodded sympathetically. He wanted her to keep talking.

'His Mam said he'd got parole for good behaviour and he's coming home tomorrow.'

'Does he live around here.'

'In that white house among the trees.'

Mike knew he'd have to warn the family. Having committed two murders and attempted another Mrs Brown wouldn't stop now. He drove to the house and rang the bell. There was no reply.

Back at the guesthouse Mike rang directory enquiries. The number wasn't listed. There was nothing else for it but to go back the following day and warn the family in person. He took a quick look at the website. The youth had been moved to first place, ahead of Greenacres Pharmaceuticals, so he hadn't much time. His own case had risen too but he'd worry about that later.

Next morning he drove to the village again. There was nobody at home in the white house. Perhaps the parents had gone to collect the lad from prison. The house was at the end of a lane bounded by thick hedges.

Mike climbed the stile into the field opposite. He'd brought his field glasses with him. He'd pretend to be a bird watcher and the glasses would help to hide his face if Mrs Brown came by.

After watching for a while he saw a figure in a flowery dress walk up the drive and emerge a few minutes later. She walked away in the opposite direction then doubled back along a lane that came out behind the house.

Mike ran to the house and looked through the letterbox - no sign of fire, thank goodness. He walked all around the outside. The windows were closed and there was no sign of illegal entry. There was a garage at the back. Both doors had been left open. He went inside.

He came out fast. The whole place smelt of petrol and there were splashes of liquid everywhere. Mrs Brown would only have to throw in a match and the garage would go up in flames.

He sprinted across the green to a phone box.

'Somebody's poured petrol all over a garage and is hiding ready to ignite it.'

The police believed him this time. They said they would be along at once. He raced back to the house just as a car turned into the drive. He shouted, but the driver didn't hear him. Suddenly a figure in a flowery dress ran out holding a flaming wad of paper.

Mike grabbed her arm and felt the flame brush his face as he knocked the torch to the ground.

She grabbed at his throat. 'Murderers!' She screamed.

He tried to shout a warning but he couldn't. He pulled at her hands, amazed at her strength. Obscenities poured from her mouth. He realised that she was quite, quite mad.

The family alighted from the car to stand in stunned silence, unable to comprehend the scene in front of them. Then police arrived, but even they had difficulty in subduing Mrs Brown.

They found she had no accomplices. Guard Dog was hers and hers alone. When they checked the rest of the list they found that as well as the murders, she'd committed several crimes of vandalism and criminal damage. She'd learnt a lot from her years as a magistrate.

Thank goodness that's over, Mike thought, pouring himself a drink from the bottle his neighbours had left for him on the porch. They always remembered his birthday.

Funny, it tasted a bit odd. He took another sip, ugh, horrible. He wouldn't have any more. He'd go and make himself a nice cup…

The Scandalous Three

'We're never going to get published at this rate. I've written to five publishers all specialising in romantic novels and every one of them has sent it back with a tatty printed slip saying they don't accept unsolicited manuscripts.' Penny shook her fair curls angrily.

It was the first meeting of the creative writing class since the summer break and the friends had agreed to meet in the canteen afterwards, hoping to have some good news to report.

'I've had no results either,' said Kirsty, unless you count a pile of slips saying "Sorry, not suitable for our list." I don't know what is suitable for their lists if a crime novel written by a police officer isn't suitable for publishers specialising in whodunits. They didn't even read the covering letters. I know because I dusted them for fingerprints.'

The others gazed at her in awe.

'I knew they never read them,' said Janet indignantly.

'I'm sure nobody's read mine – apart from the one who scribbled "Sorry we don't do humour" on the bottom of my letter prior to returning it.'

They consumed their drinks gloomily.

'The only way to get published these days is to be famous in the first place, or come out with a rip-roaring scandal and sell it to the highest bidder. I bet if I said I'd had an affair with Prince Charles they'd be queuing up to publish it.' Janet never could be serious for long.

'I dare you!' said Penny, getting into the mood. 'Though I think Prince Charles is a bit old hat by now.'

'Yes, but he's not the only prince, is he,' said Kirsty. 'He's got brothers, sons, cousins – even a dad. And of course there's lots more princes kicking around Europe. Why not just say we had an affair with Prince X and let them all just guess who it was?'

'Yes, then they couldn't do us for libel.' Janet, more mature than the others, always thought of the consequences before she did anything.

The silly exchange had cheered them up. They agreed that instead of writing an exercise for class next week each one would write her own outline of a royal scandal, then compare notes over coffee.

They had a good giggle when they met again. Penny had written a tender romance ending in heartbreak when Prince X dutifully returned to his wife and new baby. Janet had written a cynical but very funny story of a prince trying to have an affair, but thwarted at every step by inquisitive journalists, an over-protective mother and a private detective terrified of losing his job. Kirsty, drawing on her police experience, had written a scurrilous account of a foreign prince's pursuit of a call-girl through the sleazier night spots of London.

'I reckon we ought to join forces and really write the book,' said Janet. 'Let's get together one weekend and work it all out.'

The idea matured and within a few weeks the story was finished. They had some difficulty in finding a title but eventually agreed upon "Prince's Rhapsody".

The story concerned Prince X, who had become attracted to a waitress he'd met in a London night-club. Despite many difficulties they managed to meet in secret and become lovers. They exchanged promises. He gave her presents and an apartment in Paris, but then he tired of her and left her heartbroken and penniless in a foreign city.

Kirsty wanted to have him murdered but the others refused.

'We're trying to get the book published. The only way we're ever going to get a publisher to look at it is to convince him the story's real,' Janet reminded her.

'We'd better decide who's going to be the author before we send it,' said Penny. 'It can't be me because my husband would object.'

'And I can't risk my job,' said Kirsty. 'They aren't very keen on that sort of thing in the police force. It'll have to be Janet. She's her own boss since the divorce.

She's on her own since the boys went away to university so there's nobody to ask nosy questions about the mail and she hasn't got a job so she can't lose it. We'll have to think of a good pen name for her.'

'Let's call her Janine Delanoir,' suggested Penny. 'It sounds glamorous and if the postman notices a different name on the letters he'll just assume someone's spelt Janet Delaney wrongly.'

Penny, who had been a secretary and had the best word-processor, typed the manuscript. Janet had more time on her hands than the others so she toured the book-shops looking for publishers specialising in gossip and scandal. She wrote to several but received the usual disappointing responses. Then, out of the blue, she received a letter from a publisher she was sure she hadn't written to. Excitedly, she telephoned Penny with the news.

'I've had a letter from an Asil Bhadmoggi of Bhadmoggi Publishing. He wants to see the full manuscript. I've never heard of him. He's not in the yearbook.'

'It's probably some editor who's broken away to set up on his own and taken a few manuscripts from the slush pile with him.'

'He wants me to go and see him in London but I can't. He'd never believe someone of my age had had an affair with a prince.'

'I can't go. I couldn't get back in time to get the children out of school. Besides my husband would

160

want to know what I was doing in London. It'll have to be Kirsty; she looks quite nice when she's not in uniform and she can always get a weekday off if she's had to do a weekend.'

Kirsty agreed to go. She was a little surprised when she arrived at the publisher's office to find no doormen or secretaries; just a foreign looking man sitting at a large desk in a sparsely-furnished room. He said he represented a middle eastern publisher who specialised in royal genealogies but who wanted to spread his wings into more general royalty-interest books. He liked her manuscript, he said, and was prepared to offer £100,000 for full copyright. Janet recovered her wits just in time to tell him to make the cheque out to her real name before Mr Bhadmoggi showed her briskly to the door. There was no chat, no pleasantries, not even a cup of coffee. From the cafe opposite, she saw him leave the office almost immediately and hail a taxi.

They waited eagerly for publication but as the months went by they heard no more about the book. Letters to the publisher were returned stamped "unknown at this address" and attempts to telephone Mr Bhadmoggi met with the number disconnected tone.

'You'd think the scandal would have hit the headlines by now,' said Penny, some months after the meeting. 'I don't think they're going to publish it.'

'I'm rather glad actually, I'd been imagining all

sorts of problems that could have arisen.' Janet's maturity had reasserted itself once the euphoria of being accepted for publication had worn off.

'The cheque's cleared so at least we've got the money to do what we like with, though I'd still rather be a real author.' Penny smiled wistfully.

They continued to attend classes. Penny had a short story accepted by a woman's magazine and Kirsty started to write another crime novel. Kirsty had to do a lot of overtime that term and couldn't always get to class, but she made sure she met up with Penny and Janet over coffee afterwards.

One evening, after a particularly interesting talk from a writer who had self-published his own novel, they arrived for coffee to find her excitedly poring over a photograph in a gossip magazine she'd found lying on the table.

'Look!' she said. 'That's him, Bhadmoggi!'

'It says he's Sheikh Ghlassali,' said Janet.

'I know it's Asil Bhadmoggi. I'd know him anywhere by that double wart on his chin.'

'It says here he's the foreign minister of Abu Dhotti, seen here with his friend and cousin Prince Xashmak, the current favourite to inherit the throne.'

'Prince X!' cried Penny excitedly. 'I'd never have guessed there was a real one. They must have thought that's whom we meant!'

Kirsty read the article out to the others. The oil-rich Sultan of Abu Dhotti had been diagnosed with inoperable cancer and was being pressed by his ministers to name his successor. His eldest son the crown prince, unwilling to wait for nature to take its course, had attempted to speed up matters by engineering a coup, only to be discovered in time and beheaded. Two of his brothers were playboys, and therefore unacceptable to the religious faction, and his half-brothers were far too young. Prince Xashmak seemed to be the only son suitable and his case was being supported by his cousin and friend Ghlassali, who was heavily tipped to become Prime Minister if Xashmak became Sultan.

'Now I understand,' said Janet. 'Sheikh Ghlassali must have heard of our manuscript via a contact in one of the publishing houses, thought we were referring to Prince Xashmak, and decided to buy the story to suppress it.'

'I'm relieved. I'd never felt easy at the thought of that thing being published. Someone might just have found out it was us.' Penny had always worried that her husband might find out she'd helped to write a scurrilous book.

It was some time before they heard anything of Abu Dhotti again. Then the Sultan died and was succeeded by Prince Xashmak, who appointed someone they'd never heard of as his Prime Minister. Nothing more was heard of Sheik Ghlassali.

Then suddenly, out of the blue, the scandal exploded. A book published in Arabic claimed that the new

Sultan had had a steamy affair with an English waitress. He denied it of course, but he was dethroned all the same and his cousin Ghlassali became the New Sultan. Now director and sole owner of a vast oil industry, Ghlassali must have felt that £100,000 was a small sum to pay for the privilege.

Janet, Penny and Kirsty are now published authors. It had turned out to be very easy after all. Inspired by the speaker, who'd published his own book, they used Ghlassali's cheque to set up their own publishing company. There was sufficient money to pay for the editing, printing and publicity of the three books, and even have some left over for printing a few rejection slips.

As Kirsty put it, 'There's no point in having your own publishing business if you have to sit there and read other people's boring old manuscripts, is there?'

The Studio

The sole topic of conversation was the exhibition. Only three weeks away now, the students were putting their final efforts into producing pictures good enough to hang.

'What do you think is your best picture?' Asked Mavis.

'Blackhall Rocks. I've nearly finished it, though I'll have to go down again and check on one of the arches. I've got it all out of perspective.'

Len came over to the table and hesitantly asked if he could join them. A shy youth, Alex wasn't sure that she liked him. It wasn't easy to get him to join in the conversation.

'Space is getting to be a problem now,' Mavis continued. 'I don't know how you manage in that poky bedsit of yours.'

'I don't have to worry anymore,' Alex grinned. 'I've hired a studio.'

'Hired a studio? You must be mad; how on earth can you afford it? '

'Not easily, but at only fifty pounds a month it's cheaper than getting a bigger flat.'

'Where is the studio?'

'At Mrs Farrington-Gurney's place. It's that big red brick house on the Ryhope Road, right on the edge of town. The studio's over the garage. Mrs Farrington-Gurney said it used to be the coachman's flat when the garage was the coach house. Her son used it as a studio before he went to Australia.'

'Aubrey Farrington-Gurney; I don't like him, he's nasty.' Len joined in the conversation for the first time.

'Why don't you like him, Len?' Alex asked.

'My name's Leonard, not Len,' he shouted, jumping to his feet. 'I don't like being called Len, I'm Leonard.' He stamped out of the refectory, still calling 'I'm Leonard,' over his shoulder from the corridor.

'My, what's the matter with him Mavis?'

'I don't know. We always called him Len at school. He's been mentally ill, you know. He always was a bit withdrawn, but he was a smashing artist. The art teacher entered him for the inter-schools prize and everybody expected him to win it. Then his mother died and he just dropped out of things. Nobody saw him for ages then we heard he'd been in a mental hospital.'

She finished her drink.

'Aubrey was entered for the prize as well. I think he won it, so Len might have been feeling a bit jealous.'

'Mrs F-G seems to think her son's the greatest artist since Picasso. She said he'd had this big exhibition in London where all the critics raved over him. Then he took it to Australia and they persuaded him to stay. I don't think I've ever seen anything of his. What sort of an artist is he?'

'I didn't know him well, he left when I was in the fifth form; but I seem to remember his pictures being big and brash, and frankly, rather gruesome.'

'What, spooks and churchyards and things?'

'No, cruel things, like women falling down stairs, or getting drowned. I heard the head telling his mother on parents' evening that Aubrey was too preoccupied with the macabre, but Mrs F-G wouldn't hear of it. "My son's a very fine artist and I won't have his creativity interfered with," she said.'

They put their mugs down and returned to class. Len had taken himself off into a corner and wouldn't look up as they entered. He didn't speak to them again for some days, even though Alex made a point of calling him Leonard. She even asked him if he'd like to join them in the bar for drink on her birthday but he just said a curt 'no thanks,' and rode off noisily on his motor bike.

Alex didn't have time to worry about Len and his problems because she was too busy getting ready for the exhibition. A week before it was due to open, a policewoman came to address the class.

'Don't go out painting alone in remote places,' she said. 'Go out in a group if you must. A woman artist disappeared last week and bits of her body turned up yesterday in black plastic bags on a disused factory site – we're still looking for the rest of her. Then another woman, out bird watching, said a man had tried to slink up behind her, but fortunately somebody came past walking a dog. When she reported the incident she said there was a land rover on the track.

'Do be careful. If it's the man we think it is he's very dangerous. He's shown all the hallmarks of the serial killer we had two years ago; the land-rover, the mutilation of the victims and bits of dismembered bodies left all over the place in black dustbin bags.'

'Do you mean the Hilton Hacker?' Asked one of the students. 'I thought he was dead.'

'We thought so too. A man committed suicide and left a note confessing to the murders, but a few of the things he said didn't add up. We now think he was just some disturbed character imagining himself to be a famous criminal, and the real killer's still out there. Maybe he's had the sense to lie low for a while, or perhaps even been in prison for another crime.'

'Or mental hospital,' muttered Mavis.

'But he's out now and murdering again,' continued the policewoman. 'So no risk-taking please.'

'Maybe you shouldn't be alone in that studio,' Mavis said afterwards.

'Oh the studio's all right. The bus stops at the end of the drive and there's a jolly good lock on the door. Besides, Mrs Farrington-Gurney's usually around.'

'Do you see much of her?'

'Very little. But she's usually in the house; I often hear her radio.'

'What's she like?'

'Obsessed with her son. Apparently Aubrey kept everything spotless so I'm expected to keep everything spotless too. There's this lobby thing, before you go into the studio, and it's absolutely full of cleaning materials.'

'What is it like as an art room?'

'Terrific! It's got lots of space and light, a big old-fashioned sink and a massive deal table I can use for my framing. There's loads of cupboards too and I can use any of them except one that's got some things of her son's in it and that one's locked anyhow. If I sell a few paintings at the exhibition I might keep the studio on permanently. It's wonderful to have somewhere to spread your things out and just leave them while you get on with something else.'

'Like having a meal off the table!'

Alex laughed. After a year of trying to combine art with living in a tiny bedsit the studio was a luxury she was determined to hang on to as long as possible. It had good electric lighting too and she often worked late, taking the last bus back into town.

Len became friendlier as the date of the exhibition approached; though he could still withdraw into himself if anything upset him. His own work was exquisite. He painted delicate flower studies in watercolour, and Alex could well understand how he must have resented missing the inter-schools prize. He offered to accompany her when she said she'd have to go back to Blackhall Rocks, but she said she'd already arranged to go with Mavis.

'I wouldn't go off alone with him,' Mavis muttered when she told her.

Blackhall Rocks was duly finished and Alex thought

it was the best painting she had ever done. Big and bold, it had a depth and liveliness she'd never managed to achieve before. She packed it carefully and took it to her studio to frame it.

Some hours later, she stood back and admired her handiwork. It really was a lovely picture. She'd put it in the exhibition but mark it "Not For Sale." She wasn't going to part with this one.

She went to the cupboard for the entry form she'd carefully propped up behind a pile of pastel boxes. She couldn't see it.

'Drat, where's it gone,' she muttered to herself. She moved the boxes aside but still couldn't find the form. 'I know I put it in here.'

She had taken most of the boxes out of the cupboard before she found it; a tiny corner of white paper sticking up from the crack at the back where it had slipped down into the cupboard beneath.

She took hold of it to pull it out, but as soon as she touched it, it slid further down. Then when she tried to manoeuvre it out with her palette knife it dropped down out of sight altogether.

'Blast, it's gone into the locked cupboard. I wonder if Mrs Farrington-Gurney has the key. Maybe she'd unlock it if I asked her.'

But Mrs Farrington-Gurney wasn't in. The house was in darkness. Alex had to take that form in to college tomorrow if she was to put anything in the exhibition. Could she pick the lock? She'd heard that people could do it with a credit card. She didn't have a credit card, but perhaps the palette knife would do instead.

She picked up her palette knife and slid it gently between the door and the jamb. She felt the resistance as it met the lock, then as she continued to push, the lock clicked back and the cupboard door swung open.

Alex sprang back with a cry, for instead of the art materials she had been expecting, she saw a great row of carving knives, and a steel and a cleaver; all hung up neatly on hooks, highly polished and shining in the lamplight. And at the bottom of the cupboard was a roll of black polythene bin-bags.

She screamed. Everything fitted now. Brought up to think he was perfect, and with an obsession with depicting violent accidents to women, Aubrey Farrington-Gurney was the perfect suspect for the role of the Hilton Hacker. When things got too hot for him he'd gone to Australia. Now he was back, and murdering again. Sick at the thought of what he'd probably been doing on the table she'd just been using, she ran to the sink and retched helplessly, then leant against the wall trembling.

What should she do? She tried to collect herself and think. She'd have to lock the cupboard again of course. Aubrey must never know she'd seen what he kept there. She'd try it to see if she could lock it with the palette knife. She placed the knife against the lock and sighed with relief as it clicked into place. Then she picked up her bag and prepared to leave.

She'd ring her father in the morning and ask him to come up with his car and help her take everything out of the studio. She never wanted to see the place again. Alex was just about to lock up when she heard a vehicle approaching. She glanced out of the window. A land rover was coming up the drive!

Had he seen her? She drew back and watched from behind the curtain as a man got out and went into the house. He had his own keys.

Waiting only to make sure he'd shut the door behind him, she tiptoed down the steps, then darted into the bushes bordering the house. She'd left the light on in the studio. He must have seen it as he drove up – let him think she was still there. It would give her more time to escape.

Watching the house door all the time, she stooped down, moving from shadow to shadow, trying to get to the road before the man came out again. She heard the door open and shrank down behind a shrub, watching as he mounted the steps to the studio. He opened the door quietly, then went in and closed it behind him.

She didn't wait to see what happened next, just sprinted up the drive towards the road. She heard a muffled oath and a crash as the studio door slammed against the wall, then a thudding of feet on the wooden stair and a pounding and panting on the drive behind her.

The road, The road! She must get to the road! She could see the lights ahead of her and hear the rushing of the cars.

A coarse hand grabbed at her arm. She screamed, and twisted away. Then he caught her again and crushed her against him. Something cold and hard pressed against her throat.

I'm going to die, she thought.

Then suddenly, he let go of her and stepped back, as a bright light advanced upon them. She heard the roar of a motor bike, and as she reeled away from it, saw the helmeted figure of the rider lean over and strike at the man who had been holding her.

'Quick, get on the bike behind me. I can't keep him off for long.' It was Len's voice.

Tremblingly she mounted. The man lurched towards them. She saw a gleam of metal swinging towards Len's face. Len ducked, and the bike swerved wildly across the gravel; then accelerated away out of danger.

Len took her to his aunt; the aunt he'd lived with since his mother died. She looked after Alex while Len phoned the police.

'How did you know?' Alex asked as soon a she had time to speak to Len again.

'I saw Aubrey in town yesterday. I recognised him immediately. He was getting into a land rover and I knew then that he must be the killer. There was a man in hospital just like him. He used to draw pictures of women being injured and he was always tormenting frogs and things. I went to the police but I don't think they believed me. They knew I'd been ill, you see. So I went to your flat to warn you, and when you weren't in, I reckoned you must be here. Aubrey won't get far. I got his registration number and gave it to the police. They'll have to believe me this time.'

'I don't know how to thank you, Leonard,' she said.

'You can call me Len if you like. I don't mind. I'm better now.'

Thunder on the Levels

There was a flash of lightning as I turned into Long Drove. The sky grew darker and I could hear a rumble of thunder in the distance. Then suddenly, there was sheeting rain, obscuring the windscreen and rattling on the roof like bullets.

I switched on the headlamps. The light gleamed on water overflowing the rhynes and spreading out half way across the road. The rhynes – those drainage ditches that accompany every track across the Somerset Levels – were wide and deep and sometimes sheep drowned in them. One false turn of the wheel and the car would be in the water and me with it – possibly trapped for hours. I should have turned back then and taken another road, for I knew that if the light failed I would have difficulty in keeping to the track. But the floods had turned every gateway to a sea of mud ready to engulf my wheels, and the floodwaters obscured the little bridges, so I couldn't see where they ended and the ditches began. There was literally, nowhere to turn.

I could only drive on slowly and hope to hold the car steady for the two miles I knew I had to go before reaching higher ground. The storm was overhead now and flashes of forked lightning lit up the sky. At least the lightning showed up the road better, I thought wryly. I supposed that if the worst came to the worst, I could simply stop. But then I might meet up with another vehicle and didn't at all fancy trying to reverse to the nearest passing place, if indeed there was still such a thing amidst all the encroaching water.

A particularly lurid flash showed a group of huddled figures hurrying along the Drove towards me, before they disappeared into the gloom again. Should I offer them a lift? There seemed to be so many of them. Perhaps I could just take the women and children. I didn't really want to, as I didn't like the look of them. Despite the lack of visibility I'd got the impression they were disreputable in some way, though to be fair, I supposed I'd look disreputable if I'd been out in all that rain.

Another flash of lightning confirmed my impression. Squat and tangle-haired, there was a shambling looseness about their gait, which combined with a posture so suggestive of aggressive watchfulness that any feelings of obligation to play Good Samaritan evaporated at once. I decided to drive on however unhappy the children looked.

I could make out the figures now, seven or eight of

them. The impression of disreputableness increased. Glastonbury attracts many so-called travellers and people of weird persuasions, but most of them are harmless. The group approaching me on the road didn't look harmless at all.

The next flash of lightning showed the approaching travellers in some detail. They were smallish people, with matted hair, clad in some sort of informal garments. They looked, I thought uncharitably, as though they'd just taken up a pile of old rugs and flung them round themselves and they didn't seem to be wearing anything underneath. And they were undoubtedly carrying spears.

It was the spears that frightened me, for all of the people, even the children, were carrying them, holding them out in front of themselves as though ready for attack. Hastily I locked the car doors and was determined not to stop whatever the persuasion. Vagrants, hippies, didycoys, even outright drug addicts don't carry spears. Whatever they were I didn't want to know them.

I drove forward slowly and sounded the horn. That was a mistake. With howls and yells I could hear even over the raging storm, they charged the car, hurling their spears, which made great clangs and screeches as they hit and scraped across the metal.

The people were all around me now. I could see them clearly; filthy animal faces contorted with hatred; obscenely hairy arms battering and slashing at the windscreen. Terrified and sickened, I trod on the accelerator and drove straight through the gang; they would have to leap aside or be run over. They jumped, and when I glanced in the driving mirror they were running down Long Drove behind me. The next bolt of lightning showed them running across the fields towards Glastonbury Tor. I cried out in alarm, for there was no building on the top of the Tor!

Floods or no floods, I accelerated and drove as fast as possible towards the village and safety. Never before had I so longed for the comforts and amenities of civilisation.

Sam was sympathetic, but I don't think he really believed me. 'They were probably another bunch of travellers,' he said when I told him what had happened. He handed me a cup of tea and tried to convince me that I'd had a bad fright and imagined things to be worse than they were.

'They weren't travellers. They weren't any of the local weirdoes either. Their faces were different – almost ape like, with that heavy look about their foreheads. And they were all horribly bandy-legged.'

'Vitamin deficiency. I expect they've all been brought up in some cranky community that doesn't believe in eating properly and they've all got rickets.' Sam had no time for people with dietary obsessions.

He went out to examine the car, exclaiming angrily at the dents and scratches on the bonnet. The storm had gone as suddenly as it had come and a watery sun showed up gleams of bare metal where the spears had scraped it.

'Hello, what's this?' He prised out what looked like a piece of gravel from one of the windscreen wipers. 'Why, I do believe it's flint! Surely they weren't carrying flint-tipped weapons? I wonder if they were film extras or something – or one of those groups who have agreed to live like people did in the olden days, so as to make a television series?'

'People from a television series wouldn't have attacked a car.'

He had to agree. We debated the matter for some time but I knew Sam didn't really believe I'd seen all the things I said I'd seen. He can be like that sometimes. Anything he can't understand can't have happened. He was particularly insistent that I couldn't have seen Glastonbury Tor without its tower on top.

'You couldn't have been looking properly,' he said. 'The hippies scared you witless and you were half-blinded by the lightning and the rain. There must have been a building on top of the Tor. St Michael's Chapel has been there for over seven hundred years.'

'Maybe it got struck by lightning and fell down,' I said. I knew I wasn't wrong about the tower. Frightened and dazzled I may have been, but there's nothing wrong with my eyesight.

'Then we'll find out when we pass it tonight when we go to David's lecture,' Sam said.

David was the Vicar's son, doing a PhD in Archaeology at Bath University. He had been excavating near Glastonbury, hoping to find evidence of more Iron Age settlements. I didn't really want to go out again after my hazardous drive that afternoon, but David was popular in the village and the lecture was in aid of church funds, so I thought I ought to go.

'See, the tower is still there,' said Sam as we drove past.

I said nothing. I knew it hadn't been there when I looked last time. We entered the hall, greeting friends and acquaintances. Sam went over to his friend Mac from Neighbourhood Watch and told him that a crowd of unkempt travellers had attacked the car on Long Drove. Mac said we ought to report it to the community policeman, and get the people, whoever they were, moved on before they did any more damage.

'They must have just moved into the area,' he added, 'for he didn't mention travellers at all at the meeting last night. He's usually very good at letting us know when suspect groups move in.'

I didn't take in much of David's lecture, at first. The events of the afternoon had tired me and my attention was wandering, till I was brought back to full wakefulness by a muffled exclamation from Sam beside me.

'...some evidence that the settlement near Long Drove might not be Iron Age at all, but a relic of the Stone Age – a good three thousand years earlier than we had expected.' I heard David's young voice clearly describing his finds.

'We found signs of an ancient trackway, running along part of what is now Long Drove, then veering off across the marshes towards Glastonbury Tor. We carried on excavating and found some flint tools – scrapers and spearheads mostly. Then we really struck it lucky. There was this lovely big boggy patch; acid enough to preserve some of the organic artefacts these people must have used. We found several long straight pieces of wood, grooved to take flint spear-heads, and even bits of dressed animal hide. It seems our ancient friends went about dressed in wolf skins and carrying spears.'

Sam and I glanced at each other, then he gave a disbelieving shake of the head.

David continued. 'As we dug deeper, we found traces of the people themselves, first a thigh bone; a very bowed and bandy-legged thigh bone, then a piece of bone from a human skull. The skull was particularly interesting. It showed the front of the face with the massive brow ridge of Late Palaeolithic man. There were signs of a sharp fracture and some charring, and at first we thought the owner had been killed with a club and his body was burnt afterwards. But when we sent it for forensic testing, the pathologist said the edge of the fracture was too sharp to have been made by a blunt instrument. Something much more powerful hit the man, and charred his skull at the same time. He came to the conclusion that our Palaeolithic friend had been struck by lightning as he trotted along beside Long Drove.'

I've never gone along Long Drove again. I always take the longer way round now, when I'm coming back from Glastonbury. Sam has never admitted that he believes I met a bunch of Stone Age travellers, that stormy afternoon last May, but I've noticed he always takes the long way round too...

The Fairy in the Greenhouse

There was a fairy in my greenhouse, sitting on the shelf. I thought at first he was an ornament somebody had put there for a joke.

'My, you're lifelike,' I said reaching out to take hold of him.

'Of course I'm lifelike, I'm alive!' he said indignantly, jumping out of reach.

I covered my face with my hands, blinked rapidly and looked at the shelf again. He was still there.

'My name's Cocoa,' he said.

It suited him for he was brown from head to toe; brown eyes, brown hair, brown shirt and leggings, and the most delightful chocolate coloured leather jerkin and boots.

'What are you doing in my greenhouse?' I said unsteadily.

'I'm on community service and I'm here to help.'

I didn't want a fairy in my greenhouse. I didn't

believe in them. Maybe if I ignored him he'd go away. I turned to leave.

'I can help you win at the show,' he said.

I hesitated. I wanted to show my pelargoniums, but whitefly last year and a late frost the year before had ruined my best specimens. This year I was determined to succeed.

'What can you do? You're far too little to lift the watering cans or the plant pots. Wouldn't it be better to do your community service somewhere else?'

'Oh don't say that! If you send me away the Queen'll think I've annoyed you and she'll turn me into a toad or something. I'm a gardener and can do skilled jobs a lot better than you can. Please let me stay. I'll be really helpful.'

'Why are you doing community service, Cocoa?'
He looked guilty. 'I got drunk and the Queen caught me.'

I laughed. The thought of that tiny being rolling around the place singing was irresistibly funny. Cocoa laughed too. He had an appealing laugh and I couldn't help liking him. Surely nobody that small could cause me any serious problems.

So Cocoa stayed and he was a real help with anything requiring skill or delicacy. His tiny hands made neat work of the disbudding and he was a wonderful pesticide, soaring and diving after the whitefly like a spitfire after a messerschmidtt. But most of all he enjoyed deadheading. He'd fly about with his little chopper singing Gilbert and Sullivan songs in that slightly cracked tenor of his, then he'd turn round and grin at me and bow.

He sang constantly, and as I liked Gilbert and Sullivan too we'd often sing duets as we worked.

He could act too, and his rendering of "Here's a how-de-do" was the funniest thing I've ever seen. He'd race around the staging pretending to drive a very old car, revving noisily and changing gears with a fearful jerk.

I wondered if I ought to offer him lunch, but when I asked he said he always brought his own. He showed me his minute sandwich box and tiny flask. I teased him about the flask.

'I hope there's nothing alcoholic in there.'

He looked alarmed. 'I wouldn't dare. The Queen would be furious if she found out.'

'And turn you into a toad?' I joked.

'Don't say things like that. She'd really do it if she was cross enough.'

The Fairy Queen herself couldn't have faulted the way Cocoa worked. The greenhouse blossomed and I had plants good enough to show in all the major classes. The night before the show I selected the best from each category and got them ready for loading. They looked so lovely I could have kissed them.

Next morning I bounced out of bed, dressed quickly and dashed into the greenhouse to say hello to my darlings.

I screamed. Every plant had been beheaded and

flowers lay dying all over the floor. Who could possibly have done this? A rival? Surely nobody from our friendly local society would have done such a thing.

I heard a snore from behind a flowerpot. I pulled it aside and there was Cocoa, asleep with his mouth open, an empty bottle beside him and a strong smell of alcohol in the air.

'Cocoa!' I shouted. 'Did you do this?'

Cocoa sat up and eyed me blearily. 'Behold the Lord High Executioner,' he sang, swinging an imaginary axe.

'Cocoa! You beheaded all my flowers!'

'With a cheap and chippy chopper and a big black block.' He carolled. 'Defer-er, defer-er to the Lord High Exec...Execush....' He had some difficulty with the word.

I should have known. I should have guessed that with a name like Cocoa (more likely spelt Ko-Ko), a passion for Gilbert and Sullivan and an obsession with deadheading, every time he got drunk he'd be bound to go around chopping heads off.

'Is that why the Queen punished you?' I demanded. 'Did you behead all the Queen's flowers?'

He grinned. 'Yes, and the King's too.' He burst into song again. 'A life long lock, a short sharp shock....'

I grabbed him before he could finish. 'I'll short sharp shock you, you little murderer. I'll cure your drunkenness once and for all.' And, with that, I picked him up, dunked him into the watering can and held him under till he stopped wriggling. Then I threw his body onto the compost heap and covered it up with a pile of grass cuttings. I felt no remorse; he'd richly deserved it. And they couldn't prosecute you for killing a fairy. Could you imagine a police officer or a high court judge actually admitting he believed in them?

I set to to clean up the greenhouse, almost crying as I swept up the debris of my hopes. Then I noticed one plant still in bloom, in a corner behind the bucket. I pulled it out and inspected it; it was quite perfect and covered in bloom. Ironically the variety was called 'Fairy Queen'. Maybe Ko-Ko was too much in awe of this lady to mutilate a plant named after her. I was too angry then, to wonder whether I should be in awe of her myself. There was still time to go to the show if I hurried, so I packed the plant, and drove quickly to the hall.

My Fairy Queen won every class it entered. I won best Pelargonium, best Angel Pelargonium, the novice cup, best local member and Best In Show. The Chairman himself came over to congratulate me. Never before in the history of the show, he said, had a novice won the Best In Show.

I drove home with silver cups rattling in the boot and my head in a whirl. Then I began to feel uneasy, realising for the first time the seriousness of what I'd done. Perhaps one really could be prosecuted for killing a fairy. I'd have to make sure nobody found the body. I'd dig him up and put him in the incinerator as soon as I got home.

But by the time I reached home, I couldn't bear the thought of looking at the body. It was too early to light the incinerator, the neighbours might object. I'd do it after tea. I put the car away and put the kettle on.

As I was making the tea I heard something tapping at the window. The tapping continued. I looked up and nearly spilt hot water on myself, for there, hovering outside the pane, was a small winged figure, knocking on the glass trying to attract my attention.

'Let me in,' said a voice obviously used to giving orders.

The Fairy Queen! My heart sank into my boots. If she'd found out I'd murdered one of her subjects what would she do to me? Would she cast a spell and turn me into a toad?

Hastily, I opened the window and curtseyed deeply, awaiting the worst.

'May I sit down,' she said graciously?

I upturned an eggcup and placed it on the table. I thought of offering her tea but couldn't think of anything small enough to serve it in. Besides, if she knew I'd killed Ko-Ko there'd be no way of placating her. I'd better keep quiet and not risk annoying her further.

'I'm so sorry that Ko-Ko ruined your plants,' she said.

I started, and wondered what she was going to say next.

'My husband and I are very cross with him. This is not the first time he's been drunk and destructive. He used to work in the royal gardens till he beheaded all the spring bulbs. We said we'd give him one more chance, and if he performed his community service conscientiously he could have his job back. We really thought he'd learnt his lesson.

'Then when he didn't report in this morning I sent a page to look for him, and he found your plants ruined and Ko-Ko hiding in the compost heap. He must have fallen into a water butt or something; he was soaked to the skin. It's lucky for him that fairies are immortal, for if he'd been human he'd have drowned. He's feeling very sorry for himself now, and when he's fully recovered we'll think of some suitable punishment for him.

'I can't apologise enough for what he's done to your poor plants and I'd like to make it up to you if I can. Is there anything you'd really like, – something you can't easily do for yourself?'

I thought hard. What could I ask for? It wouldn't do to be too greedy. Perhaps I'd better ask for something I wanted for the garden. Maybe she had a spell for repelling slugs.

'That's most kind of you Ma'am,' I replied. 'Can you do anything about the slugs? They're ruining my lettuces.'

'Slugs? Oh yes I know just the thing for getting rid of slugs. Leave it to me.' Then with a wave of her hand she flew out of the window.

I collected my wits then went down the garden to pick

a lettuce for my tea. I hoped the slugs had left me one. Everything had turned out for the best. Ko-Ko wasn't dead and I'd won the prize for best in show. I was feeling quite cheerful again. 'Here's a how-de-do,' I sang to myself.

'Urgg a urgg-ug-ug,' echoed a croaking voice from the salad bed. It did it again. Something seemed to be trying to accompany me.

I bent down and peered between the plants. There, with a slug between its paws, sat a large black toad.

The Little Cowsbury Chamber of Commerce Choir

'We've got to do something about the war memorial, Vicar. People are starting to complain.'

'I've been to the council, Gally, but they won't do anything. They say it's not their job.'

Gally carried on filling up the Vicar's car. 'But so many people are upset, their dad's and granddad's names are on it.'

The Vicar couldn't suggest anything. Gally Gallon raised the matter again with Frank Middens when the farmer came for his diesel.

'What we wants is a parish council,' said Frank. 'You can get all sorts done if you has a parish council. They gets a share of the council tax.'

'Well we can't. The vicar before Mr Chasuble came tried to get us our own parish council but the man from the ministry said we couldn't have it.'

'What can't we have?' said little Miss Stamp from the post office, who had just driven up in her mini.

'We can't have no parish council,' retorted Frank angrily. 'Bureaucracy I calls it. We pays out taxes doesn't we?'

'I expect it's because the population isn't big enough. Anyway, why do you want a parish council?'

'To get the money to repair the war memorial of course.'

'Mmm.' Miss Stamp thought for a while. The two men waited respectfully. She'd been a school-teacher in London before she came to the village and they were a little in awe of her.

'I know what,' she said. 'Why don't we have a Chamber of Commerce? There's more than enough of us for that.'

'Isn't that a bit high falutin' for a place like Little Cowsbury?' Gally shook his head doubtfully.

'I don't see why. I think you just have to get a lot of business people together and start it.'

'I thinks it's a good idea,' chipped in Frank Middens. 'Ain't we always reading in the paper about Market Dreeping's chamber of commerce doing this and that? If we had a proper chamber of commerce maybe they'd listen to us.'

'Shall I ask the other business people what they think?' Gally said. 'I can catch them when they come to have their cars filled up.'

The others agreed. Miss Stamp promised to mention it to people in the post office and Frank Middens said he'd raise the matter in the pub. Before the week was out everybody who had any claim to be in business had been appraised of the idea.

'We'll hold a meeting,' said Sam Spigot. 'You can hold it in my pub outside of opening hours.'

'Oh yeah? So's you can sell us all a lot more beer.' Sometimes Frank Middens was a little too personal.

Sam ignored him. 'I thought of asking the Vicar to come. He can chair it and keep order.'

'The Vicar's not in business; unless you means the business of saving souls.'

'He can be the chaplain,' retorted Sam shortly. He didn't like Frank Middens. Frank's boots put the other customers off. He'd tried putting a boot scraper outside the pub door with a notice saying 'PLEASE WIPE YOUR FEET' but Frank usually ignored it.

The Vicar thought it was an excellent idea. 'I'll ask my wife to make some posters,' he said. Mrs Chasuble agreed. They looked very effective.

Gally put one up on the garage forecourt, Frank Middens nailed one on the farm gate, Miss Stamp put one up in the Post Office and the Vicar pinned one to the parish notice board. The Spigots displayed one in the bar and several on the pub windows. Soon everybody in the village was talking about it.

The first meeting was well attended. In addition to Frank, Gally, Miss Stamp and the Spigots, there were the Battersbys from the fish and chip shop and Les Chimbley the sweep. Sam spigot served everybody with a free pint and the Vicar took the chair.

Public Meeting

To found a Chamber of Commerce

**Cowsbury Arms.
Tuesday 3.00 pm.**

Only self-employed people need attend.

'Is everybody agreed that we want a chamber of commerce?'

'Aye Aye,' they said.

'Is it agreed that my wife shall be honorary secretary and Miss Stamp treasurer?'

Everybody agreed with that too; nobody else wanted to do the work.

There was a stir as a latecomer arrived. Mrs Floorcluff, the pub's charlady and general help to all those who could afford her, came in as soon as she'd finished washing the glasses. Sam Spigot looked disapproving.

'What are you doing here, you're not in business?'

'Oo sez I'm not in bizniss. I'm self employed, ain't I?'

'Yes but that's not proper business.'

'Do you want your floors scrubbin' or don't you?' said the charlady angrily.'

'Of course you're eligible Mrs Floorcluff,' interjected Mrs Chasuble hastily. The vicarage had very large floors.

'I'd like to bring my Billy along,' said Mrs Battersby diffidently. 'I know he's not very bright, but he does a nice job mowing people's lawns and it would do him good to feel he was a proper businessman.'

'I'm sure he'd be very welcome,' said The Vicar. The vicarage had absolutely enormous lawns.

The Chamber of Commerce lost no time in sending a letter to the council, asking for a grant to repairing the war memorial and the chairman, secretary and treasurer were invited to a meeting in County Hall. They were impressed. The County Treasurer and his assistant were so charming that it was some time before the Little Cowsbury contingent realised that they'd been fobbed off.

'No grant then,' said Miss Stamp angrily as they made their way back down the staircase. 'I should have known better than to trust a local government officer to talk straight.'

'Smarmy bastard,' said Mrs Chasuble feelingly. The other two pretended not to hear but they were glad she'd said it all the same.

They made their way towards the door. Suddenly, Miss Stamp stopped and pointed. 'Oh look,' she said. 'They're holding the county music festival next month and there's a thousand pound prize for the best choir. Why don't we enter the competition and win the money to repair the war memorial. I used to run the school choir,' she added. 'There's some very good singers in Little Cowsbury. We could win if we really tried.'

'You're right,' said Mrs Chasuble. 'The hymn singing's always very good. Why don't we get the Chamber of Commerce to organise a choir? I can play for them and Miss Stamp can conduct. We could use the church to rehearse in, couldn't we dear?'

'Oh yes, certainly.' The Vicar was in favour of anything that brought more people into church.

The Chamber of Commerce agreed unanimously to found a choir. Those who liked singing were enthusiastic, those who didn't know if they could sing or not agreed to try and those who couldn't sing at all came along to make helpful comments.

As rehearsals got under way it became obvious that they would have to cast their nets wider than the Chamber of Commerce. 'Let's ask Barry Mudlugs,' said Mrs Chasuble. 'He's by far the best singer in the parish.'

''Ee's only a farm labourer,' cried Frank Middens indignantly. ''Ee's not self-employed.'

'Then he can be a co-opted member,' said Mrs Chasuble firmly.

'My Billy's a good singer too,' said Mrs Battersby. 'They did a lot of music at his school and he got the prize for singing every year.'

The Vicar, Billy and Barry formed the nucleus of the men's section, and were able to help the weaker members. Mrs Floorcluff turned out to have a surprisingly good voice and Miss Stamp made her lead soprano. Mesdames Chimbley, Gallon and Battersby could sing quite well and co-opted a couple of friends and before long, the church was echoing to the sounds of enthusiastic singing. They had chosen a medley from 'The Pirates of Penzance' for their competition piece. The school in the next village had done it the year before and lent them the music.

There was great excitement on competition day. The ladies wore pretty dresses and the men wore their Sunday suits. Mrs Chasuble even persuaded Frank Middens to leave his dirty boots at home, though she had to give him a pair of shoes from the parish jumble sale before he'd agree to abandon them.

The choir did well, but they didn't win. The prize went to a bigger group with much more experience. They did however receive a commendation for the best novice entrant.

'That won't repair the war memorial,' said Frank Middens feelingly, as they sat watching the winners go up to the dais to collect their awards.

'No, but it was jolly good fun,' said Mrs Floorcluff, giving him a playful dig on the arm. Frank blushed.

He was trying to pluck up courage to ask her to go to the pictures with him.

''Ere look, there's Miss Stamp talking to a man.'

The postmistress was standing at the back of the hall chatting enthusiastically with a distinguished looking gentleman.

'Wasn't he the leader of one of the other choirs?'

'Well 'ooever 'ee is I think there's summat goin' on there,' she giggled.

Miss Stamp brought the man over and introduced him as a colleague from her teaching days. He'd got tired of teaching in London, he said, and had left to become an insurance broker.

'Do you make a lot of money?' said Frank Middens.

'Really Frank.' Miss Stamp gave him her best schoolmistress frown.

'I help other people make the most of their money,' he replied with a smile.

'Then maybe you could advise us how to get the money to pay for repairing our war memorial.'

The Vicar took charge. He explained the situation to Miss Stamp's friend, who seemed to be amused by the story.

'What a long-winded way to achieve a very simple thing,' he said. 'How did the war memorial come to be damaged?'

'A tree blew down on it in the gales.'

'Did the tree belong to anybody?'

'It was it was in Mrs Floorcluff's garden.'

'Then Mrs Floorcluff's responsible for renovating the memorial.'

''Ere. 'Oo are yer accusin' of bein' responsible?' Mrs Floorcluff was not going to be blamed for anything.

'Mrs Floorcluff couldn't possibly pay for the war memorial, she's a widow,' said the Vicar hastily.

'Oh I don't mean pay for it herself. She can claim it on the house insurance.'

'My 'ouse insurance? But the tree was not in the 'ouse it was in the garden.'

'Most policies cover the gardens too. If you let me have a look at it I can sort it out for you.' He smiled at Miss Stamp, clearly hoping for an invitation to come to tea with her at the same time.

She gave it. The following Sunday Miss Stamp's long-lost friend, having sorted out Mrs Floorcluff's insurance policy, accompanied the ladies to Evensong. He spoke to the Vicar afterwards.

'I'm thinking of moving out here,' he said. 'You have some very fine male voices in your parish. I've always wanted to start a barbers shop quartet but I've never been able to get four good men living near enough to rehearse together. Would you care to join it Vicar?'

The Vicar said he would be delighted.

'And those other two splendid singers in your choir?'

The Vicar had no difficulty in persuading Barry Mudlugs and Billy Battersby to join, and next year, the Little Cowsbury Chamber of Commerce Barbers Shop Quartet won the prize for the best quartet; the best male voice ensemble and the cup for most points overall. They took home a lot of prize money.

They bought Billy Battersby a new motor mower and some hedge clippers, so he could expand his business. Barry Mudlugs asked for a state-of-the-art hen house and he now sells his eggs and can honestly call himself a businessman. The Vicar put his share in the church roof repairs fund.

'Isn't that a bit too unselfish of you Vicar?' asked Gally Gallon.

'No. I'm sick of having water running down my neck when I'm preaching. But what are you going to spend your share on Leader? You've done so much for everybody else.'

The man who had brought prosperity to little Cowsbury put his arm around Miss Stamp.

'I'm going to spend it on a diamond ring for my fiancée,' he said.

Doing the Business

Bernard was shocked, shocked to the core. They couldn't sack him; not after all he'd done for the company. Five years of faithful service and all that unpaid overtime and they had the nerve to tell him they were having to cut back and he would have to go.

'Can you wait a moment here please? The director would like a word with you,' the receptionist had said. He'd waited, but he hadn't seen the director. It was Aubrey his own assistant, the man he'd trained up from nothing, who'd come skittering down the stairs to hand him his possessions in a carrier bag and tell him he wasn't allowed back into his own office any more. The young upstart was smirking. 'I'm taking over your job,' he said.

It all made sense now; that play that was acted out two years ago. They'd upgraded him because of his knowledge of client data systems, then shortly after, they'd called him in and offered him his boss's job.

'Don't ask,' they'd said when he'd enquired why the older man had left. 'There are some things it's better we don't discuss.' He'd assumed then that there'd been an impropriety the company didn't want to reveal for fear of losing clients.

'Of course things are a bit tight after what's happened, so we won't be able to increase your salary. Still, you're a bright chap and when you've helped us get on our feet again we'll see what we can do for you.'

Well he'd helped them get on their feet again (if indeed they'd ever been off them) and frankly, he'd done a better job than his old boss. He'd saved the company thousands of pounds though the promised salary increase had not been forthcoming.

'Times are bad,' they'd said when he'd hinted that perhaps it was time for a rise. He realised then that getting rid of his predecessor had been merely a ruse to get the same job done for less, and now they'd played the same trick on him. He stood in the car park dazed and shaking, very conscious of all the eyes looking down at him from the windows. Soon everybody would know he'd been sacked.

He felt a surge of anger when he realised that if anyone enquired, they'd hint that he'd done something he shouldn't. They'd cheerfully destroy his character just to make sure nobody learnt of their dirty little tricks. Well they wouldn't get away with it. He'd get even; he'd hit them where it hurt. He'd destroy the client database – the lifeblood of the company. He'd use his manager's key and come in after hours and wipe it completely.

Slamming the car door he drove home fast, made a pot of coffee which he forgot to drink and applied himself to enjoying the idea of destroying his erstwhile employers. He'd have to look for another job of course, but he would do that after he'd taken his revenge.

The doorbell rang. It was the director's secretary, smiling up at him from he doormat.

'I've come to give you your cheque,' she said, handing him an envelope. 'And I think you forgot to give back your keys.' She continued to smile until he found them in his briefcase and handed them over.

They'd foiled his little plot, the suspicious so-and-so's, but when he opened the envelope and saw that they'd given him the minimum one month's salary, he was even more determined to get even.

He'd have to get into the office when the building was open. That shouldn't be difficult; there were always people coming and going. The problem was that if he were recognised he'd be thrown out.

He thought a while. Maybe he could slip in through the fire escape door during the weekly staff meeting. He knew that the typists often left it open for fresh air and forgot to shut it when they left the room. If anyone apprehended him he'd simply say he'd left his spare door keys in the filing cabinet.

Next meeting day he parked behind the building next

to his old employers and watched the windows until he'd seen his former colleagues leave their desks to go to the conference room. With his heart thundering against his ribs, he walked through the adjacent lots. The fire door was open and suppressing the urge to run, he climbed steadily up the iron staircase to the typing pool. A quick check showed the corridor to be empty and holding his breath he walked along it to his old office.

The door wouldn't open. That little rat Aubrey must have locked it!

Perhaps he could force the lock; he'd heard you could do it with a credit card. Better use his library card though; he couldn't risk breaking what was fast becoming his only source of income. He tried to wriggle the card between the lock and the door jamb but nothing happened. Blast! He remembered too late that he'd insisted on having a deadlock fitted. He'd have to find another way. He made his way out through the pool again, spitefully tipping some water from a flower vase into one of the word-processors as he passed.

Thinking about it back home, he remembered that the central heating engineers were due to come and test the system some weekend soon. It should be easy enough to get in then. He rang the engineers, pretending to be from his old company.

'Can you confirm which weekend you're coming,' he said. 'I think my secretary may have got it down wrongly.'

'This weekend,' they replied. 'We come the same weekend every year.'

He prepared his campaign carefully. He'd have to make sure the caretaker didn't recognise him. What a pity he hadn't had time to grow a beard; he'd have to wear a false one. He scanned the yellow pages till he found a theatrical costumier, then went to buy his disguise.

It was easy to get into the building. He chose the time the caretaker usually went for his tea and walked in through the front door. He carried a clipboard, so if any of the engineers saw him they'd assume he was from the company and if anyone from the company noticed him they'd just assume he was a foreman sent to supervise the engineers. He ran up the stairs to what used to be his office and found the door open.

Sitting down at the desk as though he had every right to be there, he switched on the computer and waited impatiently for it to boot up. Then he tried to get into the database and couldn't. Blast, they'd changed the password! Well never mind, he'd simply crash the computer and destroy everything on it. A few keystrokes and it was done. He chuckled gleefully to himself. Now for the backup discs in the cabinet by the door. It was locked, of course, but he'd brought a hammer and chisel with him and a quick tap had it open.

The discs weren't there. Drat! That Aubrey must have decided to keep them somewhere else. He was just about to search the office when he heard the familiar tread of the caretaker in the corridor. Hastily he bent down to look at the radiator, then having pretended to scribble something on his clip-board, stood up and walked swiftly out of the building.

He'd think of something else, but meanwhile, he'd have to look for employment. The final salary cheque was fast running out. It was on one of his interviews that he got the idea. Waiting his turn outside the manager's office, he saw a woman with a basket going from desk to desk selling sandwiches.

'Who's she?' he said.

'That's the sandwich lady. She comes in every day and it saves us going out for lunch.'

It was a service that would have been very welcome where Bernard used to work. There was nothing but a greasy little café on that industrial estate.

He could kill two birds with one stone. He'd make a living selling sandwiches and find a way to get even with his old company at the same time! He'd grown a real beard now; they'd never recognise him. Even his own mother hadn't known him when he'd gone home for the weekend.

He drafted a notice saying 'The Sandwich Man is Coming' then ran off copies on his computer and left them at every office on the estate. He used his credit card to buy a white overall and cap, and a large basket from the catering suppliers. Then all he had do was go down to the supermarket every morning to buy rolls and fillings, and make them up before lunchtime. He became expert at finding interesting fillings and devising new combinations – it was his executive brain working overtime – and he was soon making a living. Of course it wasn't a very good living but it paid the rent and on a bad day, he could at least eat the rolls he hadn't managed to sell.

He was welcomed enthusiastically at his old firm and nobody recognised him behind the facial hair. He tried to stay away from those who had been his closest colleagues at first, but he needn't have worried; they were too busy thinking of their stomachs to notice the man carrying the basket.

It was some weeks before he attempted to get at the database. The leave rota hung where it had always hung, and he planned to strike while Aubrey was away. He'd observed him often enough now to know where he kept the backup discs. He'd take no chances this time. He'd carry a full set of tools under the white cloth lining his basket, and he'd make sure nobody interrupted him while he worked.

The day Aubrey started his holiday Bernard pounced. Waiting till the corridor was empty he hit the fire alarm, then dodged into the office and shut the door. He smiled as he heard one of the passers-by complaining. 'Blast, just when the sandwich man's coming. We'll have starved to death by the time this fire drill's over.'

In the rush to clear the building somebody had left the

cabinet open. Swiftly, Bernard extracted the back up discs and hid them at the bottom of his basket. He pressed a few keys to crash the computer and for good measure, unscrewed the back and tipped a few drops of orange juice into it. Then trotting briskly down the back stairs, he went out to dispense rolls and cartons of drink to the staff assembled in the car park.

He threw the disks in the river on the way home.

Bernard heard nothing for a while, though he knew the company couldn't last long without its database. His sandwich business was booming and he was getting requests to call from all over the town. He'd soon have to take on an assistant to cope with the extra demand and bang would go all his profit.

He was sitting trying to decide how to answer this thorny question when the phone rang. It was his old boss.

'Bernard old chap, how are you getting on? We haven't heard anything from you for a while.'

'Oh,' said Bernard carefully. He wasn't sure why they wanted to speak to him. Could somebody have recognised him beneath his disguise? His stomach lurched at the thought of what might happen to him if his act of wilful destruction was recognised.

'We wondered if you'd reconsider your decision to leave us.'

'Reconsider my decision?' Bernard wasn't aware that he'd made any decision.

'Perhaps we could tempt you to come back again.'

'Come back again?' Bernard felt increasingly bewildered.

'Would you like to come back to your old job? We'd double your salary of course.'

'But what about Aubrey?'

'Aubrey went off and got another job without telling us and you're the only other person who knows how to operate the system.'

Bernard's heart leapt; his old job back and double the salary!

Then he suddenly remembered, he'd just destroyed the company…

Jenny Cheshire

ECHOES OF THE PAST

'In this gripping and haunting love story, Jenny Cheshire has confirmed her rich talent as a first-class storyteller.'
Award-winning journalist and author Robert Beaumont

Alone and emotionally scarred after the birth of her still-born baby, Nelle is shocked to find herself whisked off on holiday to the coast of Wales by Jack, a charismatic and impulsive city financier.

But as Jack soon becomes sidetracked by boats, booze and blokish behaviour, Nelle continues to be tormented by a tragic secret. And why is she so mysteriously haunted by the ruined house at the end of the bay?

When salvation arrives in the attractive but reserved shape of Brad, Nelle suddenly finds her life in great danger. In a terrifying climax, she discovers that only by learning the truth behind their troubled pasts, can she and Brad finally conquer their demons.

But will they be allowed to?

ISBN 0-9538452-0-6

Simon Parish

CLOSED SEASON

A tragic accident and the disappearance of a close friend are seemingly unrelated events, yet they lead two people on a long and tortuous trail with a disturbing conclusion. The story is told by Philippa, whose own life is not without its trials and tribulations. CLOSED SEASON is a fast-moving crime adventure story, superbly crafted by this talented author.

An extract

I met Rebecca Waters on my first day at Oxford. It was her feet which first entered my field of vision as I bumped up the stairs with my heavy suitcase, then the sturdy legs pushed into tight jeans followed by a generous bust and finally, as I reached the top stair, an even more generous smile.

"Hello, I'm Beck."

"Phil," I volunteered, gasping for breath, "Philippa James."

"Here, let me give you a hand," with which she relieved me of my case and proceeded to help unload the car, assembling a growing pile of belongings in my room; a simple act of kindness yet typical, as I came to learn, of a warm and giving nature. I took a liking to Beck straight away.

ISBN 0-9538452-1-4

Simon Parish

FINAL BALANCE

Forced retirement and a series of malicious attacks trigger off a chain of events which carry the seeds of tragedy for ex-banker George Phillips. On the trail of the perpetrators is ambitious, young local reporter, Julie Wright, who stumbles on a serious scam and inadvertently finds herself in danger…

A gripping story of our time

George wasn't quite sure what Anthony was talking about. He sat expressionless, still clutching the near-full cup of coffee which was rapidly going cold.

"Our bank isn't insensitive to the impact these developments will have on the structure of the industry and it has publicly declared its intention to become a major player now we've crossed the threshold into the new millennium. In my view, we shall not just be participants in this revolution, we shall be at the cutting edge. It promises to be an exciting time."

Anthony's voice had risen by several tones and his eyes were fixed on a distant point, somewhere above and to the right of George's head. They came back into focus and sought George's own face which remained unmoved by the prospect of this new, golden age.

"Which brings us to you, George."

ISBN 0-9538452-3-0

Bolero

Crime

Mystery

Romance

*Bolero books can be ordered through
your local bookshop*